About the Author

An eager reader and writer from an early age, it wasn't until she first discovered Jane Austen that she found her passion for historical fiction. She immersed herself in the Regency culture, the feasts, the dancing, the balls and the customs. She enjoys combining her love of historical works with inspiration from her own life and experience.

E & M

L K Smith

E & M

Olympia Publishers
London

www.olympiapublishers.com
OLYMPIA PAPERBACK EDITION

A CIP catalogue record for this title is
available from the British Library.

ISBN: 978-1-78830-622-5

First Published in 2020

Olympia Publishers
Tallis House
2 Tallis Street
London
EC4Y 0AB
Printed in Great Britain

Dedication

To my mother, Anita, for her regular attentions to my efforts, and my very dear friend, Naomi Penney, for her faithful encouragement and her willingness to read.

Preface

This book is set in the growing and newly industrial village of Reading, Berkshire, and begins in the March of the year 1816. The streets and references to actual places are as near to accurate as much as maps and knowledge with a distance of two hundred years will allow and should not be taken as certain if you happen upon them in that time.

Chapter One

"My dear Mariah," said Edward to his sister one day, "you must congratulate me!"

"Congratulate you, Edward?" She smiled and looked in his direction. "Have I a sister at last?"

"Indeed, you have! And you will never guess who, for this very day, I met with her mother."

"Oh Edward, you are not serious, of course I should guess who, has she not dined with us every week since Christmas? I believe even our dear old aunt could guess your news." Edward smiled and nodded. It had not been every week, but in his elation, he would cheerfully bear her teasing.

"So you approve?"

Mariah nodded. "Have you spoken with Aunt Mary?"

"Ah, I thought it fitting that I should speak with you first. But of course, I will speak with our aunt directly."

The banns were read, and Edward's betrothed called on Mariah at her home the week before her impending marriage.

"I am so happy for you and Edward; I am pleased we are to be sisters at last," said Mariah to Elizabeth.

"Oh, exactly so, my dear," said her guest, viewing around her soon-to-be home with a fresh eye. "Hmm. This is a fine house; however, I do believe these walls need redressing, some new paintings perhaps. Oh, do not worry, for I have excellent taste on that score. As its new mistress, I shall bring this terrace into the modern style. But I really do think, that is to say, do you not think the house too small for so many people?”

“Addison Terrace?” said Mariah, surprised, and with a little laugh added, “It is hardly small. For surely eight bedrooms, two of which are very large, two parlours, a large drawing room, a dining hall, an impressive library and study for a town house is more than enough rooms for four.”

“Oh indeed, there will be four, but when you and your aunt visit there will be six of us, so you must be sure not to visit us too often or we shall be overrun,” said Elizabeth with a little laugh.

“This is a new idea, but six?” asked Mariah.

“Oh, it was all settled a month ago. But yes, my dear, four of us, as my mother and younger sister are to live with us next month. She will pay her own way, of course. My mother is to lease out Partridge Lodge.” She smiled sweetly and continued, “She has no need of such a large house. She would only have my younger sister with her, and she would be ever so lonely such a way off.”

Mariah nodded slowly and thought Elizabeth very strange, for she knew that Partridge Lodge was not a mile from Addison Terrace.

“But surely the grounds at Partridge Lodge are worth preserving.”

“Bless you, my dear, but of course they are, and the groundskeeper is to maintain them as before.”

“And where would you have me go?” asked Mariah frowning. “Addison Terrace is my home!”

"Oh quite, but now that you are nearly twenty-seven, you must not expect your brother to keep you all the days of your life. You are so sensible and reasonable a young woman, and I am sure no one would expect so very much from their brother. Especially once he is married, he will have such uses for his time and money that can ill afford a spinster sister. Oh, do not worry, for I am sure we will find you lodgings suitable to your economy. I understand your mother's inheritance was a considerable sum." Mariah was shocked by her daring nerve, but bore it all, only raising her eyebrows once.

"And my aunt? She is eighty-four, surely you would not wish to resettle her elsewhere?"

To Mariah and Edward, Great-Aunt Mary had always been more than an aunt. Their own mother had died when they were young children, and their father being utterly heartbroken by the loss of his wife for many, many years after, never remarried. Aunt Mary, though shorter and more slender than either Edward or Mariah, was as dear to them all as any mother would be, and with her usual quick step was always there to smooth the way.

"Goodness, I had no notion she was so very old, I expect she won't notice much at her age, but I am sure she will welcome a change of scenery. I dare say, she has had it good all these years; your brother is so generous, but you can spoil a person, you know."

Mariah felt this too much and meant to speak to her brother as soon as he returned. Their own father was, earlier this April, only two years gone; she was sure HE would never consider his duty to his family as unwelcome charity. Mariah, incensed by her presumption, though it was natural she would be its mistress, had thought her plans were beyond reasonable and changed the topic lest she speak out of turn to her soon-to-be sister.

"I hear your young sister is to be bridesmaid."

"Yes." She smiled sweetly. "Sophia is full young at thirteen to be so, but she is such a lively pretty girl, and really I do not think there is any need for more than one."

"Oh, of course, I am sure it will be everything that is charming."

***

"Edward?" said Mariah the next morning at breakfast to her brother. He was of reasonable height to be called a well-looking man, and had good fashion sense, and unlike the popular dandy, Edward was a man of business and practical style, preferring trousers and a plain brocade to pantaloons and bright silks.

"Yes?" replied he, looking up from his letter.

"I must speak with you before Aunt Mary joins us, for I do not wish to upset her, and as you well know she always joins us for breakfast at quarter to ten."

"What is it? I see you have something on your mind that is urgent."

"Elizabeth called on me yesterday."

"Did she really? That is good news, for I desire for you to both be on the best of terms."

"Indeed, Edward, that too is what I hoped. But she had such ideas!"

"Oh, I expect she is just a little excited about the wedding; it is only six days away."

"If it were merely that, I could forgive everything. But it was not."

"You are worried then… If it is that her mother and sister are to stay with us, let me assure you that they are very amiable and I am sure they will respect you as my sister."

"Oh Edward, she wishes to send me away! And Aunt Mary too. She said that I am to live off mother's inheritance and live somewhere else and rarely visit because the house will be overrun. Because I am nearly twenty-seven, but this is my home," said she. "Tell me it isn't true."

"Only for a little while, dear Mariah, while we are newly married, surely London or Bath would do for a season. I know how much you love London. But using mother's inheritance is out of the question; I shall increase your allowance. You are not to mind the expense; I will look after you. And of course, I only suggested your aunt as a companion, for she loves London as much as you do. But I never intended for it to be a permanent arrangement. Perhaps you misunderstood her. Quite right, quite right, Addison Terrace will always be your home unless you marry. And as for our dear Aunt Mary, this house will always be her home."

"I should hope so, Edward, I would be very sorry if it were not," chimed in Aunt Mary as she joined them at breakfast.

"As would I," said he.

After these events, Mariah felt relieved to be spared the duty of bridesmaid. For though a London made, peach silk gown would be most elegant and complement her colour, to her prudence it seemed too high a price and she hoped that her brother was right.

She began to suspect her new sister of duplicity. Her anxiety for herself and her aunt, however, only increased when, the day before the wedding, Elizabeth, with bold audacity, called on her again while Edward was out. In the street, her tall thin frame, fine silk coat and intensely feathered bonnet were discernible from the parlour window.

"I'm afraid you find me all alone this morning, Elizabeth; my brother and aunt are out," said Mariah with all politeness.

"Oh, I know very well that they are gone out, my dear, for it is you I have come to see," replied she.

"Well, this is kind of you to call, though I am surprised. I did think you would have too many claims on your time to see me."

"Oh, exactly so, my dear, so I shan't stay long as I do have such business to attend. It is unfortunate, and it is not quite convenient for me that I have come, but I did just want to ensure we understand each other."

"Indeed?"

"You cannot think how I was grieved to find, after our discussion last Tuesday, that I had not been taken at all seriously. I was most alarmed to find that plans had been made without my consultation—and as the new mistress of Addison Terrace you must see that I must have a say in all plans concerning its use." Though her face was stern, her tone of address still held a politeness so as not to shamelessly affront its hearer.

"Yes, that is true, you are to be its mistress, but I must have misunderstood you the other day. I believed you and Edward had already discussed my going to London… But of course, myself and Aunt Mary will go for the summer season. That is all very proper, and Aunt Mary will love it above anything. But after such time we will be looking forward to returning to Addison Terrace, as it will always be mine and Aunt Mary's home."

"I see!" Elizabeth coloured and nodded and then with a little cough added, "How strange, pardon me, I don't know how in the world you could have misunderstood me… I…"

"No matter," replied Mariah hastily lest Elizabeth's speeches became more pointed, "I am glad we understand each other now. Was there anything else? I am sorry to cut short our tête-a-tête, only I am expected elsewhere." Mariah smiled politely and stood up. Elizabeth was taken aback by the shortness of time and stood up also.

"Oh well, I expect there will be far less for you to do in future."

"Perhaps there may," replied Mariah and then led her guest to the door. "Good day, Miss Dunmead." Elizabeth accepted the hint and took her leave. But on leaving the door, she walked to the next intersection on Friar Street and stepped behind the corner wall. She did not wish to be obvious, but Elizabeth waited doubtfully to see if and when Mariah left the house.

Not two minutes after Elizabeth's departure, Mariah stepped from the doorway carrying her music book and into a waiting carriage. Elizabeth was all disappointment; she had nothing shameful to report, as Mariah had not lied.

The following day the couple were wed in the North Chapel, at St Laurence's at nine o'clock. A small procession followed the couple to Partridge Lodge, where a sumptuous wedding breakfast was held in the grounds.

"Oh, I am so happy, Elizabeth has just told me," said Sophia to Mariah after the cake was served. "We are to move to Addison Terrace next month, when they are returned."

"Yes indeed," replied Mariah.

"And we are to be sisters?" Mariah nodded. "Elizabeth said, after mother, I may have my choice of rooms on the second floor." Mariah made no reply, and wondered if this was Elizabeth's new scheme to unsettle her. "It is very large, I think. Are there many rooms to choose from?"

"No indeed," replied Mariah with a smile, "there are only four on the second floor. Aunt Mary and I have one each and after your mother that will leave only one."

"Oh well, I don't mind a jot, though I will dearly love to explore it. Does it have secret passages and nooks like dear Partridge Lodge? And is the roof space shared? Aunt Mary told me that you can see into other houses from up there."

"Yes… you can," Mariah laughed, "but it's very dark, and there is all manner of dusty old things; you might get lost, and forget which house to come back to." Sophia was suitably impressed by the oddities of her new home and Mariah supposed, unlike her elder sister, the younger would submit to its routine without any invented drama or calamity.

At two o'clock, the party broke up and Aunt Mary and Mariah took leave in the waiting carriage.

"And they are to leave tomorrow for Manchester," said Mariah to Aunt Mary when the carriage door was closed. "I only hope this good weather will hold out for them." Aunt Mary shook her head.

"Can you imagine, if Edward had listened to his wife, but thankfully, he is to take the Brougham…" Aunt Mary sighed. Mariah looked to her aunt for an explanation, which was that Elizabeth dearly wished to take the Landau, but thankfully Edward had more sense.

"They are to see our cousins in Coventry also. It has been such a time since I last saw Sir Matthew and Lady Forbes. Perhaps I should invite them for Christmas. But… no, that wouldn't be proper; Elizabeth may think me impertinent. Perhaps she will like them so much she will invite them herself." Her aunt made no reply.

"Mrs Dunmead told me this afternoon that a tenant has been found for Partridge Lodge already."

"Truly? That is fortunate, I supposed they will move in as planned then. Who is it to be?"

"Two brothers from Brighton and their uncle, there was something about a sister or cousin. But their name is Horwar, or Harvard…"

"Harward? I overheard her speaking with Dr Poole about it."

"Yes, that was it. Though I think half of Reading may have overheard her," Mariah smiled.

"Though we are unlikely to be introduced, I doubt Mrs Dunmead is the type to socialise with her tenants."

"Hmmm," replied her aunt with little interest to continue with the topic.

"And we have been invited to dine with the Matlocks tomorrow evening. However, Aunt Anna did say she would invite Mrs and Miss Sophia Dunmead also."

"Are all our social occasions from now on to include the Dunmeads?" Aunt Mary seemed almost displeased.

"Well, both Edward and Elizabeth have dined with them. It is only natural that they be acquainted with the rest of the family. They are, after all, our closest relations."

"Your mother's family? Hmm, I suppose, especially by proximity. Very well. We shall see how she behaves amongst strangers."

"Who, Aunt?"

"Mrs Dunmead!" Aunt Mary frowned. "Did you see how very familiarly she behaved with Dr Poole? Poor man, if I were him, I should avoid all connexion with… well, and with eight little ones at home and very likely more, he cannot afford to injure his reputation."

"Oh, but you forget, he attended to her late husband in his long illness. She's obviously still grieving his loss. It has been three years, and she still wears mourning clothes."

"I saw no black," said her aunt, unconvinced.

"That is true, but it was her daughter's wedding, and I have no doubt she will revert to her customary garb tomorrow."

"You surprise me! You make excuses for the mother, while the daughter tries very hard to supplant us with her own mother and sister. An apple does not fall far from the tree, my dear niece." Mariah was surprised that Aunt Mary smirked. "You think me ignorant of her schemes? Let her try me and see how far she will get."

"You will come to London with me in June, won't you?" asked Mariah, Aunt Mary nodded.

"Yes! And what's more we shall enjoy ourselves at every turn." Mariah smiled.

***

The following evening, they joined the Matlocks for dinner. Mariah's Aunt Anna and Uncle John, mildly fashionable and genteel, in their usual friendly and jovial manner, and aware of the present isolation of the ladies, invited two more families with whom they were familiar. The young Mr and Mrs Marsh and Colonel Fanning and his wife.

"And so, your daughter is married, Mrs Dunmead?" asked Colonel Fanning, a tall, thin, older man, with trim balding hair and a thick moustache that extended to his sideburns. "You must be pleased, I know I shall be, when my two have husbands." Mrs Matlock and Mrs Fanning smiled. His wife by contrast was short, plump and a mass of dark curls was visible from under her lace cap.

"You must forgive the Colonel, Mrs Dunmead, we have two daughters of our own, sixteen and seventeen, very fashionable young ladies they are," explained Mrs Fanning.

"Who think of little else," added the Colonel with a smile and a laugh.

"Say nothing of what their parents suffer in their youthful liveliness," added Mrs Dunmead in agreement.

"No indeed, nor the expense," added the Colonel with another laugh.

"Agreed," replied Mrs Dunmead smilingly. "But where are the Miss Fannings? They are not with you this evening?"

"No, they are at present with cousins in London."

"Oh, how charming," added Mariah, "Aunt Mary and I must call on them when we are in Town next month." Aunt Mary nodded in agreement.

"Marianne and Margaret will be pleased; I will be sure to mention it in my next letter," Mrs Fanning said happily. Aunt Mary then enquired after the Miss Fannings.

"And you, my dear one," asked Mrs Marsh after dinner. "How have you borne all the changes to your family life? I can see it is not so very welcome as some claim it to be." She looked over at Mrs Dunmead and Sophia. "If she says one more time how lucky Edward is, or fair Elizabeth is, I am sure my patience will be tested beyond what it can bear."

Mrs Marsh, though taller, often shadowed Mariah's own fashion and style, even in their youth, save her tight fawn curls that were always unruly.

"Of course, you mean my brother's new relations," whispered Mariah, trying not to smile.

"Perhaps I do," replied she. "I am sure she would not be so very pointed amongst her own set?"

"No," said Mariah softly, "at least not within my hearing."

"But are they as painful at home?"

"No, well, it was all going along charmingly, 'til Elizabeth wished me gone."

"No!" exclaimed Roberta.

Mariah then gave her the particulars of the conversation between herself and Elizabeth and how she had confronted her brother. Mrs Marsh was shocked and grieved that Edward's new wife may yet be found to be mercenary.

"But was there no suspicion of duplicity before the marriage?" whispered she.

"Not by me, she was everything that was perfectly charming to myself and Aunt Mary."

"How dreadful. And the mother?"

"I am not sure, Aunt Mary seems to know something, but of what I am not yet sure."

"I must admit, Mrs Norman and Lady Coburn gave me a little hint of their disappointment when Edward first took an interest in Elizabeth. But I..."

"And what are you two ladies whispering about over there?" asked Mr Matlock smilingly, but was surprised at their astonishment of being addressed and added, "Beg pardon, ladies, I meant only to ask if you would like to join us for cards." The ladies smiled in relief; they had not been overheard.

"Come to me, Roberta, darling," said Mr Marsh, "I know with you by my side I shall have all the luck."

To this, there was a general happy outcry of teasing. Roberta blushed and excused herself to join her husband at the card table.

"Ye shall not have the luck of the Irish! For I have my lucky penny. What say you to that, Mr Marsh?" said the Colonel.

"Ha! Very good, Colonel, but I'll not wager my wife for all the Chinese pennies in England!" grinned Mr Marsh.

"No indeed!" added Mrs Matlock. "And it's all very proper, sir, and you speak as you ought, for a wife loves to hear it, though it is what all newly married men should say." There was more general happy outcry before they decided to play Loo.

"How now!" cried Mr Marsh several hours later. "It is nearly eleven."

"Heavens be!" added Mrs Dunmead. "I should get Sophia home." The carriages were called and the guests waited in the foyer.

"It is very kind of you, Colonel, to take Mrs and Miss Dunmead home," said Mariah in Mrs Dunmead's hearing.

"Not at all, Miss M," said he. "The pleasure is all mine. The carriage is large enough, as you see, and if Mrs F and I bunch in on one side, there will be plenty of room."

"You are very good, Colonel," replied Mariah as he entered the carriage and left.

"You must call on us at Addison Terrace, Roberta," said Mariah quietly to her friend Mrs Marsh, who agreed that she would, and very soon.

***

Before the week was out, or Mrs Marsh had a chance to make good on her promise to call, Mrs Dunmead and Sophia called on the ladies of Addison Terrace; they had spent the morning at the markets and it was a convenient place to call in on their way home.

"Mrs Dunmead. How good of you to call on us, I see you have been to the markets?"

"Oh yes, Sophia is missing our dear Elizabeth dreadfully, but I hoped and was very much delighted to chance upon some early season gooseberries. I was quite sure it would cheer her up as they are by far Sophia's favourite. Aren't they, my dear?" Sophia nodded in agreement.

"Mm, Mama has promised me a gooseberry tart," said Sophia eagerly.

"A little gooseberry tart is a favourite of mine too," Aunt Mary said smilingly. "You were certainly lucky to get them in May… though it is late May."

"Oh, then you must call on us at Partridge Lodge this very week," declared Mrs Dunmead to Aunt Mary, eager to boast of the talents of her house. "Tarts, gooseberry tarts especially, are quite the speciality of our cook, you know… But I also had another reason for the markets, of course, from the vigneron, a special purchase of a little elderflower wine for me that is to be delivered this very afternoon."

"A successful outing then," said Mariah.

"Oh, quite favoured," said Mrs Dunmead quite impressed with her successful journey.

Mariah ordered some tea and biscuits and had only just sent the maid away when she returned to introduce Mrs Marsh. Mrs Marsh, hastily unaware that guests were already being waited on, began at once.

"Now, my dear one, before you tell me all you know on the promised subject, let me give you my invitation to our little card party Wednesday next," said she all excitement.

"A party?" asked Mrs Dunmead. Mrs Marsh looked up and immediately saw Mrs and Miss Dunmead already seated in the room.

"Oh, Mrs Dunmead, Miss Dunmead," said Roberta surprised; she smiled politely and blushed. There was nothing for it now: she must extend the invitation to the lady and her daughter. Mrs Dunmead admired the card and turned it over in her hand.

"What a pretty hand, did you write these yourself, Mrs Marsh?"

"Thank you, yes. They were my yester noon's endeavour."

"How charming," said Mrs Dunmead.

"Have you heard from the newlyweds?" asked Mrs Marsh, keen to divert the subject.

"No, but I dare say they will have other uses for their time," replied Mrs Dunmead with a smile.

Mariah agreed. "Though I am certain they have arrived in Coventry. I am sure to receive word soon." Mrs Marsh agreed that it was sure to be soon.

After tea and biscuits, Mrs Dunmead, keen for an excuse to explore the second-floor rooms, hoped Mrs Marsh's visit was a short one and waited for her to take leave, whereas Mrs Marsh, eager to discuss the subject of Dunmead, waited for the good lady to finish her tea. All the while Aunt Mary, acutely aware of the agenda of both, smiled over her tea and talked of Colonel Fanning's new carriage. Mrs Dunmead smiled and confessed that it was not quite as comfortable with four, but it was indeed a nice carriage.

Late the following week, Mariah and Aunt Mary arrived at the supper party early, so the former had time to help Roberta set up the finishing touches. The latter sat and admired the tapestries in the parlour. The little terrace was fashionable and Mrs Marsh had taken pains to modernise the parlour and have the old French tapestries repaired.

"Your aunt seems to have admired the tapestries. What do you think?" Roberta asked Mariah.

"I do like it very much; it suits the new décor much better." replied Mariah.

"I agree," said Mrs Norman, "you have a very proper talent and eye for these things, Mrs Marsh. I would have done those tapestries the most disservice."

"Surely not?" said Roberta and Mariah.

"Oh yes. Mr Norman simply could not bear anything French," replied she. She then stood up and went to speak to other guests. Roberta and Mariah tried to hide their smiles.

"Will you play for us this evening?" Roberta asked Mariah.

"Certainly, if you wish, though I haven't especially anything new," replied she.

"I take it Lady Coburn has not approached you about the recital as yet?" Mariah shook her head. "Though you are sure to be asked; you play the piano ten times better than the rest of us." Mariah smiled. "Which you know very well." Mariah grinned.

"And you flatter me too much," said Mariah with a laugh.

***

'A little while later, Mariah was approached by Mr Marsh with a gentleman she had not met before. He presented him as "my good friend, Mr Emmett Harward.

"Mr Harward that is to take possession of Partridge Lodge at the end of next month?" asked Mariah hesitantly.

"The very same," said he, smiling broadly. Mr Marsh then left them to give assistance to his wife.

"And are you here with your brothers and uncle?" asked Mariah looking around.

"Not quite as yet. Though you are right, they will be very shortly. They are to follow on in a fortnight after I have taken up lodgings at Partridge Lodge." He smiled kindly. "I did hear, the owner is to reside with you. Though I believe… this may prove to be a lucky chance for me, as we shall be near neighbours," said he smilingly. "You must be well acquainted with the family?"

"No, not at all well, that is to say, we have had very little time to be acquainted, though I am sure we soon will be."

"A small inconvenience to you and your aunt then." Mariah tried to hide her smile and nodded.

"Yes, it was a surprise, but we bear it as best as we can, sir."

"Hmm, and what game do handsome ladies, such as yourself, play in this part of the country? Are you tempted to indulge in chance? What say you to cribbage?"

"Cribbage isn't a favourite, but as the tables are set out, I suppose I ought to make an exception." She smiled.

He led her to the cribbage tables, and they sat down with several other players.

It pleased many of her company to see her so well attended by this new gentleman. And by his appearance and reputation, for he was a tall and well-dressed dandy, with gentlemanly manners and all the appearance of good breeding; they hoped that Mariah at least might desire the connexion.

Sometime later, after being less than successful at cribbage, Mariah was approached by Mrs Marsh to take a turn at the instrument.

"Mrs Dunmead is at it again, telling all my guests how lucky Edward is." Roberta tried very hard not to roll her eyes. Mariah only nodded and looked over in Mrs Dunmead's direction.

"And they are to stay at Fornavis Priory for a fortnight," said Mrs Dunmead to many listeners. "She has been quite favoured by Lady Forbes, you know."

"Are you to play for us, Miss Mariah?" asked Mrs Fanning, joining Mrs Marsh and Mariah at the instrument. Mariah nodded and smiled. "Oh, how delightful, I told my nieces and nephew, who are with us this evening, that we may be lucky enough to hear you play."

"They have come to stay with you at last?" said Mariah surprised, while Mrs Fanning was secretly trying to get the attention of her young relations.

"Oh yes, they arrived on Monday, though their stay will not be a long one, they are to join Marianne and Margaret in London in a fortnight, they are over by the Loo table with Mr Marsh." Mariah and Mrs Marsh looked over at the latter's husband. Mrs Fanning paused; her attempts to summon them had been unsuccessful. "I will introduce you later."

"Thank you. I believe I would like that very much," replied Mariah smilingly.

The music was agreed on and Mariah played with her usual superiority of skill that had long been the result of many years' perfection and talent, and in turn, was admired by many of the guests. When the applause was over, Mr Harward eagerly approached her again.

"You must allow me to say that you have made this evening a very great privilege…"

"Sir, I…" added Mariah.

"Indeed, I am in earnest, for I was not expecting such superior talent!" said Mr Harward boldly.

"Thank you, sir, but it was only two little movements," replied Mariah.

"Quite! But I have seldom had the pleasure, for music is never played in my house. Indeed, you make me quite envious of the privilege," said Mr Harward. Mariah politely smiled.

"Perhaps you are not familiar with great musicians; have you never been to a recital?"

"Indeed, I have, though Brighton is not known for its musical aptitude; there are some in London I have mildly venerated. Even so, you must allow me to admire your talent. It is far superior to anything I have yet heard."

"Thank you for the compliment, sir," replied she. "Though it is a shame you have not…" she was going to say 'not had music in your house' when he suddenly finished her sentence.

"Not played Loo! But of course, we must!" He then motioned her towards the Loo table. She almost laughed, had his face not been perfectly serious; they then sat down at the Loo table with several other guests.

"I see your card playing skills have not improved since last we met," said Colonel Fanning with a smirk.

"I see yours have, Colonel," replied Mariah.

"Yes, the devil! He's got the luck of the Irish tonight," said Doctor Poole, who threw in his cards.

"Definitely that! And some," added Mr Marsh, who also threw in his cards. "I'm out, Colonel."

"Another round?" asked the Colonel. To nobody's surprise, everyone declined.

Chapter Two

Some days later Aunt Mary was sharing her real opinion of her new relations.

"Regrettably, it is most unfortunate that your brother has aligned himself with such a family," said Aunt Mary to Mariah and Roberta, who had called on them that morning.

"Oh, it does appear to be awkward; Lady Coburn and Mrs Norman were in agonies at her constant attentions to them, by and by, they gave me such a dressing down the next day for inviting her. I explained to them that it really could not be avoided." Aunt Mary smiled as she recalled the unavoidable late invitation.

"Yes, that was most unfortunate."

"But I have learned my lesson," said Mrs Marsh more seriously. "No more hasty entrances and speeches." The ladies agreed. This was a good plan.

"But Aunt, will you not share with us what you know, for I am sure you have not told all?"

"Well, perhaps. Though audacious talk hardly warrants casting aspersions… It's not right to go blackening names of characters who are trying to make their way in the world, especially with as many starts as she's had the fortune to make." Mariah and Roberta frowned. "And, of course, if I do tell you all, then Edward might be tarnished by connexion."

"Aunt, you are enjoying this teasing, but do anything rather than hurt Edward. He is always so good to us, to me especially; he has increased my allowance, you know. Though with all the talk, Mrs Dunmead is quite capable of casting her own aspersions."

"Oh yes, did you see the frequency with which she was in Dr Poole's attentions?" added Roberta.

"Yes, Aunt Mary said so of the wedding too, but I don't think there is anything in it, I think it's because he's the only person she is really acquainted with." Aunt Mary gave a knowing nod.

"By the by, I saw Mr Harward gave his attentions to you several times."

"Yes, but I think he was attentive to everybody; he is new to everyone in the neighbourhood except your husband and yourself," said Mariah.

"Nay, Mariah, you are too modest in general, for I know his preference. He said to Mr M that he particularly liked your company and he would very much like to know you better." Mariah smiled.

"He was pleasant," replied Mariah. Roberta smiled and was even now scheming of how she might get the two of them to meet more often.

On the Sunday after the service at St Laurence's, Mariah and Aunt Mary were invited for luncheon at Chifley Grey House, the grand town house of Sir Arthur and Lady Coburn, which was, of course, gratefully accepted. Sir Arthur, a portly middle-aged man from a family of good name and noble character and the incumbent heir to a baronetcy, was everything that his reputation anticipated; he was all friendliness.

"I said to my wife yester morn that it has been many weeks since you have dined with us," said Sir Arthur to Aunt Mary and her great-niece.

"That is quite true, Sir Arthur, but let me assure you, my time has been far less pleasantly occupied; in short, I would have much preferred your company," said Aunt Mary.

"Has it really? I am sorry to hear it," replied he.

"You remember, Arty, the recent wedding of Edward and Miss Elizabeth," said Lady Coburn.

"Oh yes…" replied he. Lady Coburn smiled. There was a pause and after the dishes were served, Lady Coburn began.

"Well, I'm so glad you could join us today, as I have the most exciting news." Mariah and Aunt Mary were all attention. "As of this week, I am in receipt of purchases from London. My brother Frederick is so kind; he brought them down for me on Thursday." Lady Coburn was pleased by Mariah's eagerness and continued. "I meant to treat all the ladies of the Grey's Musical Society, so I have copies for you all."

"Oh, Lady Coburn, thank you. That is most generous, but you do spoil us," replied Mariah sincerely.

"Indeed, I do not." said she with a smile, "for I have another motive."

"Oh, yes, I recall something Mrs Marsh said on Wednesday, though she gave me no particulars, so I am all attention!" Lady Coburn was pleased that she could yet give news to her friends.

"I have finally convinced Arty, though it took very little persuasion." She looked to her husband, quite pleased with herself. "Chifley Grey House is to host a recital next month."

Both Mariah and Aunt Mary agreed that it was a charming prospect, and were anxious that it was before June twentieth, as they were for London, which Lady Coburn instantly resolved, declaring that it was to be June twelfth, in hopes that it would be a fine Wednesday.

"And have you told the Normans the good news?" asked Mariah, "Mrs Norman particularly has made no secret of wanting a new music project for some time."

"Oh, yes," Lady Coburn said happily, "she was immediately gratified by the news, and wasn't sure if she should learn the parts for the Irish flute or the oboe, to which of course I said the oboe was best, though not for the sonata."

Mariah was curious, though she was sure she already understood that the sonata was a solo piano piece. Lady Coburn immediately confirmed Mariah's suspicions with a special request for Mariah to play the first movement as a solo piece and added her assurance that it would suit her talents perfectly. Mariah could scarce refuse such an elegant and flattering request, especially as she soon made up her mind to dedicate the afternoon to its repetition, for it was doubly enticing; it was a piece she had long desired to play and Beethoven had for many years been a favourite composer.

On the third day of Mariah's revelry in music, she was joined by Mrs Marsh, who called on her at Addison Terrace. After a cautious glance around the parlour, she enquired if Mariah was alone this morning. Mariah smiled and confirmed that apart from her dear aunt she was indeed alone. Roberta looked slightly relieved and immediately began.

"You will never guess, Mr M has secured us a box at the theatre tomorrow night, it's promised to be an excellent performance, it is lately from London."

"Yes, what a wonderful scheme, I did hear there was to be a performance."

"You will join us? I know that some of these new dramas are a little daring in their motive, but all the reviews have said it is suitably moral."

"Oh, I'm not sure, would Aunt Mary approve, do you think?" said Mariah. Due to the playwright's reputation, she was unsure it was entirely appropriate.

"Of course, why should she not?" replied Roberta. "Besides, we both know Mr M would never expose me to anything wholly bad."

"That is true… perhaps you are right, I have spent far too much time in music of late. And a change is refreshing."

"Indeed, it is… so you will come?" Roberta was pleased by Mariah's reasoning and her hopes of a favourable answer were soon gratified with an affirmative certainty. The conversation then turned to the music, and the instruments for the recital, Roberta the violin and Mariah the piano.

The following evening Mariah met Mr and Mrs Marsh and Mr Harward at the theatre door. Mariah had forgotten that Mr Harward was staying with the Marshes and so was taken aback by his being one of the company. More distressed too was she by his appearance this evening, as she had thought Roberta had been a little sly. His name was not mentioned by either of them the day before. But she was grateful that she had spied them all in the distance and so had time to compose herself. She greeted them all with calm civility and taking Mr Harward's offered arm, followed the Marshes into the theatre.

On the whole, Mariah and company enjoyed the performance; it was amusing entertainment with very few occasions to blush. She was however, grateful for the brevity of the interval, for Mr and Mrs Marsh were called away by the sight of a convenient familiar face, while Mr Harward gave her every attention. He was very gentlemanly, his conversation lively and the purchased refreshment welcome, but the turn of his compliments was too studied and liberal.

The next day, Mrs Marsh was expected and dutifully called on Mariah to discuss the evening before.

"Oh, what are you reading?" asked Mrs Marsh. Mariah had just put down her Bible.

"1 Thessalonians Chapter 2."

"Oh, that was the lesson on Sunday, was it not?" asked Roberta. Mariah nodded.

"It has given me much to think on," replied she.

"Hmm…" Roberta paused and considered her friend for a brief moment but dearly wished to talk of something nearer her thoughts. "You are not questioning attending last night's performance?"

"Oh no, at least, not in that way."

"Then what is it?" asked Roberta, immediately concerned.

"Mr Harward," replied she.

"Mr Harward?" Roberta laughed. "But he is everything that is charming."

"A little too charming." Mariah nodded. Roberta looked shocked.

"Oh no, what did he say?"

"Nothing too shocking, I assure you, but it was too much."

"Never… You are overscrupulous, surely." Roberta pondered for a moment "Perhaps, he is a little eager, but he admitted to Mr M he means to get your attention, for he is quite taken with you."

"But we have only met the once. Is that not strange? I have never known love to be the work of a moment on first meeting, but infatuation, well." Mariah almost scoffed.

"Who said anything about love? It is admiration only and some men are a little more forward, I suppose. Take your brother, for instance, he'd only known Miss Elizabeth a three month before they were engaged."

"Yes indeed, but I have yet to be made entirely happy about the match. I believe there are more secrets than she would wish us to know. And my brother was so devastated by the loss of his former betrothed, I believe his new attachment has been too hasty. And from what Aunt Mary has hinted, he may yet regret the connexion."

"Dear Isabella, she was a beloved creature," sighed Roberta.

"Certainly, she was," agreed Mariah.

"How strange your aunt has spoken of it too. Isabella's aunt and uncle, I mean Mr and Mrs Norman, of course, thought that Edward was throwing himself away. I believe Mr Norman at one point took Edward aside and had words when he learned of the engagement."

"Yes, I did know. Edward was made most unhappy by the interference, and of course, he would not change his mind," Mariah sighed. "I confess at the time, I thought Elizabeth though not ideal, pleasant enough—until she expected me to leave my home."

"Oh yes. Thankfully, your brother would not do such a thing."

"Quite!"

"But, do you really think she would do it?" asked Roberta hesitantly.

"From what I have witnessed from that day to this? I would say she may privately consider it, but I do not think she would be so beastly if it came to it; especially without Edward's support."

There was silence for several moments; the ladies each engaged in their own thoughts.

"By the by," said Roberta suddenly, "has your mail come?" Mariah looked confused. "What I mean is have you received the invitation to the ball I sent you?" Mariah smiled and thanked Roberta. "I knew as you have not been out much of late that you were unlikely to meet with one, so I asked that it be sent you here."

"Oh, that is very kind of you. Yes, I am very much looking forward to it. I am so pleased it is before we leave for London."

"Oh, yes. But who shall you dance with? Is your estimation of Mr Harward so very bad, have I altered your opinion of him?" Roberta asked at length. "At least he deserves another chance, surely? As you say, you have only met twice."

"Oh, of course." Mariah smiled. "I'll not be as hasty as that, but to avoid repetitions of excessive flattery, I shall always ensure a third person in the conversation…"

"Except when dancing, of course," Roberta grinned. Mariah smiled.

Over the coming weeks, Mariah met Mr Harward tolerably often, and found, to her relief and satisfaction, that he praised more than herself.

The night of the recital was approaching and Mrs Marsh was oftener at Addison Terrace than not, to practise her part with her friend, while Mrs Norman and the Reverend's wife, Mrs Green, practised at home. Except when at Chifley Grey House, where they all practised together.

"Lady Coburn," said Mrs Green, wincing. "Really, I don't think I can hit that note." Mrs Green shook her head after a third attempt of singing it through.

"Hmm," Lady Coburn agreed, "Yes, I see that now, oh well. Perhaps it ought to be omitted?"

"It is more suited to my late niece, I think," said Mrs Norman quietly, "we none of us can sing as sweet as she."

"Oh, very true," replied Roberta, "dear Isabella, she is very much missed, Mrs Norman."

"Indeed, she is," agreed Lady Coburn, "I'm afraid I quite forgot she was our only real soprano," and smiled at Mrs Norman who dabbed at her eyes. Lady Coburn then suggested that they play the piece as an instrumental in tribute to Miss Norman. The ladies agreed this was most fitting and their parts were altered to suit the scheme. Mrs Norman was so very pleased by their kindness she was almost overcome. Lady Coburn, in consideration of her friend, thought that perhaps they had practised enough that day and ordered the tea things early.

The following day and only a week before the recital, Mrs Marsh made her usual visit to Addison Terrace on her way home from the markets.

"Oh Roberta, good morning, I have just heard from Edward. I was going to write him this morning, but it can wait."

"Charming, and how is he enjoying his travels, has he written of great distances, far towns and fishing spots, or does he endlessly speak of his wife's enjoyment of great houses?"

Mariah grinned. "Not so much the latter, he writes to say Elizabeth is quite tired of travelling, and that they have decided to return home early."

"Early? Oh, how very odd, though… I suppose travel is not to everyone's taste. And when are they expected? Mr M and I must visit them, of course, when they return." Mariah nodded and told Roberta that it was to be Saturday next. Mariah expressed her gratitude at their return being after the recital and expressed that though she had no particular reason to suspect Elizabeth's interference, for she was not musical in any way, she dreaded it all the same. Roberta agreed; she too thought it for the best.

That afternoon, while alone in the parlour, Mariah wrote two letters, one in reply to her brother, and the other to her cousins, the Milcrofts in Manchester, with whom her brother and his wife had been staying.

She had not expected an immediate reply to her letters and was intrigued at receiving one so quickly. More too, as the letter she received from Mrs Milcroft, the wife of her second cousin, both shocked and grieved her exceedingly.

Saturday, June 8, Eleven o'clock, Basil Wood, near Manchester.

Dear Mariah,

I was so pleased to receive your letter; your recital sounds wonderful. I wish Angus and I could be there for the performance. But after recent events I can honestly say, quite regrettably, we are unlikely to be invited to Addison Terrace any time in the near future. You may wonder, dear cousin, why, after so many years of good relations betwixt us, that we should doubt a fond welcome at that fair abode. Though Angus and I are more than willing to overlook the offence, it is but a trifle, it seems your newest relation cannot.

It all began after the service on Sunday. Elizabeth could not find her bonnet and gloves; she had determined the maid had misplaced them, and though Annie said she had not laid eyes on them, E began to become a little hysterical. I hoped that Edward's good sense would make her see reason. But her following actions were most extraordinary; instead of waiting for them to be found, E took it upon herself to search the maid's room! And when asked, she insisted on turning the entire room over. After they were, of course, not found there, she demanded poor Edward join in her folly. Truth be told, I've never seen anything so ugly in all my life. To say I was shocked and affronted is understating the case, but for Edward's sake, I was peaceable. But lo, two days later, the footman found both gloves and bonnet on the seat in the carriage all the while. He went and showed E where they had been the entire time, and she then accused him of stealing them for his wife. I must here praise John for his goodness, as he made no reply, though a greater man would have been sorely tempted. I know it to be true as I saw it myself from an upstairs window, and the whole house heard her screams, Edward came running, and she marched off toward town. They didn't return 'til dinner and announced that they would be returning home on the morrow. I pity Edward on his choice, and I pity you this connexion. Beware, dear Mariah, where you give your heart, she may yet give you trouble.

Yours etc

C Milcroft.

PS: Anne, Sarah, Jane and Kitty are to go to Southport for the summer and send you their love and hope, as do Angus and myself, that we may yet see you at Christmas.

***

Mariah read and reread the letter. This was indeed most extraordinary. She blushed and felt awful for Edward. What mortification he had endured on behalf of his wife in so short a time and how much he grieved the connexion already could not be determined, but Mariah, though it may only be in a small way now, was certain that time would only increase his objections. Aunt Mary was soon acquainted with all that occurred. She happened upon Mariah after she had reread the letter a third time and asked her great-niece to read it aloud without leaving out any of the good bits. Aunt Mary too was shocked, though not by Elizabeth's behaviour, only by the injury it had caused.

Chapter Three

The day of the recital arrived, and the ladies of the Grey's Musical Society assembled in the hall at Chifley Grey House. The guests arrived and were seated; many of the guests were highly respected in Reading: Councillor Morris, General Oxley, Mr Alford, Lady Susan, Sir Keith and Lady Mawson and of course Reverend Green and to Mariah's surprise, Lady Coburn's own brother Frederick was one of the guests.

"Why should you be surprised, Miss Mariah?" said he, "my sister knows I am fond of music, and she is prodigiously proud of you all," he then added with a grin, "and as I have heard several reports of uncommon talent and practices all day long, she should be." Mariah grinned also and blushed at his praise and spoke of her hope that he would not be disappointed by the performance. He, of course, was doubtless he would not.

It had been many years since Mariah had any opportunity to speak with Mr Tenby; she had been nursing her sick father, and he was for Oxford. She was charmed by his agreeable nature and unassuming behaviour. Most unlike many men of consequence she had had the misfortune to meet. She smiled and considered momentarily his good qualities, handsome features and eyes and his pleasant smile, but then checked herself and the likelihood of the connexion; she was certain it would be against Lady Coburn's wishes. Mariah was then called away and took her place at the piano.

The guests were hushed, the recital began, and each lady played her part to perfection, even Mrs Norman hit every note. Mariah played the first movement of the sonata, Mrs Green and Mrs Marsh sang beautifully, and they finished with a dedication and the instrumental piece. There was an enthusiastic applause and the ladies were warmly praised for their efforts by the other guests as refreshments were served.

After the recital Lady Coburn's brother, Frederick, Mr Tenby, approached her a second time.

"I have just learned from my sister that you are for London, Saturday week."

"Yes, indeed, sir. My aunt and I are to summer in London…"

"That is capital, have you any plans for your stay?"

"Yes," replied she.

"Oh." Frederick looked slightly disappointed. "Is all your time accounted for in London? Are you staying with some acquaintance?"

"No indeed, sir," Mariah smiled. "We are staying in a favourite apartment in High Holborn Street. But we are engaged to spend time with the daughters of Colonel Fanning and their cousin's family… and my aunt is very keen to visit the museum." She paused while he nodded. "It is a favourite outing of hers and I confess, not unwelcome to myself," explained Mariah. "I understand you live in London now?"

"Yes, with my uncle in Hans Place. You may wonder at my being very forward," he paused.

"No, indeed…" smiled Mariah. Compared with Mr Harward, his behaviour could hardly be considered forward.

"It's my uncle, you see, he has card parties very often, if he is not at an evening assembly… you will think it very shocking, I am sure when I tell you… I find it a dull and tedious duty." Mariah laughed. Frederick looked surprised. "You are amused by my misfortunes?" he smiled.

"Forgive me, for I am quite of your opinion."

"Oh no, say it isn't true?" said Frederick in mock astonishment, "a lady who dislikes cards."

"It is I who am astonished sir. In my experience, a gentleman is rarely in the habit of finding it dull."

Frederick grinned. He was then called away by Lady Coburn, who was anxious that he meet some of the other guests. Mariah thought she perceived Lady Coburn's displeasure at her having taken up so much of his time, but it was gone in a moment as her attention too was called away by another guest.

Mariah had barely time to look about her when she was approached by Mr and Mrs Marsh who, being attentive to her needs, also brought her a drink.

"I am surprised at you, my dear one," said Roberta, "you have not looked for a favourite amongst us."

Mariah was confused by her implication and blushed in spite of herself; she was still thinking of Mr Tenby.

"You look conscious." Roberta looked from Mariah to Mr Marsh. "Have I said something wrong?"

"Oh no… but I can't think of whom you mean?" replied Mariah.

"Forgive us, Miss Mariah, my wife only means to point out that you have not asked after he who expressly sent you his compliments as he could not be here today." Mariah recollected herself and immediately remembered their guest.

"Oh my, yes…" She paused, then added, "I trust Mr Harward is well?"

"Yes, of course, the picture of health, well he was yesterday, he had some business in the south and could not be here today, you see," said Mrs Marsh. "Fear not, my dear one, for you are not forgot, as he has assured us he will be back in time for the ball." She grinned and looked to her husband for reassurance.

"I think he intends to solicit your hand for the first two dances," whispered Mr Marsh with a nod.

"Ha, yes, how thoughtful of him," added Mariah wincingly.

"Indeed, it is. Though it is a shame you are for London so very long." Mariah made no answer. Mrs Marsh then added in a whisper, "We don't want him to forget you, my dear, while his attentions to you are so steadfast."

"Oh, very true!" added Mr Marsh. "We may yet see you in July perhaps, and bring him with us. I am sure he will have very little objection to being seen in London."

Mariah thought them very kind and spoke politely of their plan as good, though she really wished they would not.

***

Over the next two days, Mariah made sure that the house and servants were in order for the arrival of Edward and his wife. Lists were drawn up, arrangements refreshed, rooms tidied, fireplaces cleaned and a fine dinner ordered for their arrival.

Mariah was making her way across the hall to go upstairs a third time when Aunt Mary commented from the parlour.

"Much less fuss was made for your father when he moved in fifteen years ago after his elder brother died, do you remember…? You were only eleven, I think." Mariah only nodded and made no answer; while she agreed with her great-aunt, she wished for every effort to be made to constitute the happiness of the newly married couple—it was after all their house now.

Edward and Elizabeth arrived. Edward greeted his sister and aunt warmly and then without another word, went directly to his study. Mariah hardly had time to consider his actions, before Elizabeth, frowning after him, began speaking.

"You may wonder at my surprise just now… but I am so very disappointed." Mariah and Aunt Mary both looked confused. "Oh, very well, it seems, little hints won't do." She then clutched her head in pain. "Oh, my head… I am all disappointment," said Elizabeth, shaking; she seemed to imply that this was Mariah's and Aunt Mary's fault. "I hope you will both forgive me for being direct…" winced she, then lowered her voice and added, "I had hoped you had left for London early, especially as Edward had written a week ago to tell you of our earliest arrival. Surely you understood that we would wish you gone."

"What utter nonsense!… Forgive you? Never, rudeness can never be tolerated. Your charms may have worked for a time in Manchester, Elizabeth, but we are gentle people who like peace, harmony and kindness. Whatever your wishes may be, if it is convenient to me, I will do my best to be cooperative. Mariah and I, however, will go to London on Saturday as planned." Aunt Mary then walked away. Mariah was shocked and desperately tried to hide her smile; Elizabeth was gravely silent.

"I see that you are tired from your journey," said Mariah kindly. "Why don't you let Mrs Till show you upstairs." Elizabeth nodded and followed the maid. Mariah followed Aunt Mary to the drawing room, and they sat in silence for several minutes when they heard the study door open; it was Edward.

"Oh, my goodness," wailed Edward, frowning. "What have I done to us?"

"What is it?" asked Mariah, all apprehension.

"Do not think me ignorant or blind to her treatment of others, dear Mariah… dear Aunt? It is beyond shameful. You tried to warn me, Aunt, I know, and Mariah, as did the Normans. I see that now, but what can I do?"

"Do?" asked his aunt and shook her head. "Oh, there is nothing for it now, Edward, you must abide by your choice. You must make your own happiness and be ever watchful of your wife." Edward nodded. "However… you must not let it drive you to despair, you have much to live for, many a man has married a stupider person and lived long to despise it, but you must be kind to yourself and not let one mistake mar your entire life."

Mariah, eager to relieve his present feelings, believed food to be the perfect distraction. She recommended that dinner be served directly and enquired after their cousins in Coventry and Manchester.

Elizabeth, fancying herself very ill with a dreadful headache, did not leave her room for two days. Edward, however, enjoyed the solitude while Mariah and Aunt Mary only interrupted him at mealtimes. There was peace and quietude below stairs, till Mrs Dunmead called on them and roused her eldest daughter's spirits on account of the ball.

That evening, once inside the dance hall, Mariah was immediately approached by Roberta while Edward and Elizabeth walked towards their Aunt and Uncle Matlock and Colonel Fanning.

"Now my dear one, we have brought him as promised," grinned Mrs Marsh. Mariah looked up to see a smiling Mr Harward.

"Oh, I," stuttered Mariah, "Good evening, Mr Harward," who did not wait for her to approach and immediately asked her to dance. She had not time to think and accepted his offer.

"It is not often I have the fortune to dance with someone as graceful as yourself," said Mr Harward.

"You are mistaken, sir, I dance not half so well as many other ladies you see here," replied Mariah.

"Will you allow me to say then that their understanding of the music..." he paused for the turning set and added, "their understanding is not so great as yours and therefore less graceful because of it."

"I will allow that my study of music is extensive, but I cannot agree with your notion of grace." He smiled and they went down the dance and had very little opportunity after that to speak.

Between dances, she was approached by her Aunt Anna.

"I was surprised to see Edward and Elizabeth here this evening. I wonder they have come back early, I understood they were to be away till Tuesday next..." said Mrs Matlock, while Edward and Elizabeth were dancing.

"Oh yes, did you not know? They had planned to stay longer, but it did not suit Elizabeth." Mrs Matlock only nodded. They both watched the dancers; Mr Harward was dancing for the second time that evening with Mrs Dunmead.

"However," added Mrs Matlock at length, "I did think a certain gentleman was paying you his attentions, but it seems he also gives his attentions to another." Mariah smiled. "You smile, my dear, is that the smile of admiration…?"

"Oh no," replied Mariah hastily.

"I met with Mrs Marsh yesterday, and she is of the opinion…" began Aunt Anna.

"Oh, her head is full of strange ideas at present…" interjected Mariah. Aunt Anna spied her niece with fresh curiosity.

"Pardon me, I was going to say… she is of the opinion that Mrs Dunmead has some terrible secret." Mariah relaxed a little. "But I can't imagine what that would be. Though I do hope that neither Edward nor the family are injured by it… But Mariah, you look relieved, especially as this news which ought to be distressing, seems to have had little effect on you. Pray, what other news is there to tell?" Mariah blushed, leaving her Aunt Anna, who knew Mr Harward to be staying with Mr Marsh and his wife, with little doubt that Mariah admired Mr Harward all the while. Around the same time, Mariah saw Mr Tenby arrive with his sister and brother-in-law. He acknowledged her from across the room and was directed another way by Lady Coburn who was looking for a seat.

A quarter turn later, Mariah was again momentarily distracted by Mr Tenby when she suddenly observed Mr Harward seemingly courteously, though a little awkwardly, prise himself from Mrs Dunmead and unexpectedly move in her direction. Mariah looked away immediately lest it be seen as an encouragement by him, but it was too late. Mr Harward was temerarious in his ambition and the next moment he insisted that Mariah dance the next with him. Mariah, unable to think of an excuse, cordially accepted.

They had not progressed down the dance one place before Mariah wished it had been in her power to refuse him; for he stood so close his warmth could be felt by proximity, and he could lower his voice to whispers and still be heard.

"I have a secret," whispered he. Mariah blushed to hear it.

"Sir, I beg your pardon, but…" said she.

"Tis nothing shocking, I assure you, it is only a secret because no one else yet knows, but I am determined that they shall by the end of this evening…" Mariah looked away and winced; she dearly wished she had not agreed to dance with him again. "Since you will not ask it, I will tell you; I have a wild preference for your dancing, Miss Mariah," said he, a little more loudly. And he turned her with enthusiasm. Mariah smiled politely and looked down the dance and was surprised to see Mrs Dunmead dancing with Dr Poole.

Mariah was so relieved when the dance was over that she made her way over to Roberta by the refreshments area, where it was a little quieter and slightly hidden from view of the dancers.

"My dear one, you look quite worn out," said Mrs Marsh.

"Oh no, well, a little."

"Did you see Mrs Dunmead dancing?" Mariah said that she had. "And it is quite shocking, for she has danced every dance!" Mariah looked surprised. "She has only once danced with someone else besides Dr Poole and your Mr Harward."

"It is not so very strange to be always dancing at a ball, is it?" replied Mariah teasingly.

"I suppose not, but I do think her a little strange, do not you?"

"Hmm, not really, but I do know what you mean, though I can't put my finger on it," replied Mariah, all hesitation.

Roberta nodded slowly and enquired after her brother and his wife and expressed her surprise at seeing them this evening as she quite forgot about their early return, and that she would pay the bridal visit on the morrow.

"Are you not dancing, Roberta?" asked Mariah. Roberta shook her head.

"Not in my condition," grinned she.

"Oh, that is delightful news…" Mariah said happily.

After a little while, Mariah excused herself, as she had not yet paid her respects to Lady Coburn. And Mrs Marsh soon had another companion. At length she found Lady Coburn and Sir Arthur speaking with the Reverend and Mrs Green. Before she had opportunity to speak with them, she was addressed by another.

"Pardon me, miss, I do not think we've had the pleasure this evening."

"Mr Tenby! I was just going to speak with your sister."

"Oh, never mind that, I've come to relieve you of tedium." Mariah grinned.

"Have you indeed, sir? And what do you propose, if I am indeed without diversion, as you say?"

"Without diversion? I would never presume that you are without diversion; you have danced several dances. No… only that, in my observation, it has yet brought you little pleasure."

"Oh, I… well, that is to say, opportunities were few, so I danced because I must."

"I see that you are not without flair for the diversion, so I must ask, do you enjoy dancing in general?"

"Thank you, yes, but I find there is more pleasure in it… when one's dance partner is more… agreeable."

Frederick grinned and Mariah felt that he understood perfectly her feelings.

"Then, might I tempt you to dance the next with me?" Mariah smiled and with gentle calmness agreed to dance the next with Mr Tenby.

After the dance, Mariah returned to her friend.

"He is growing on you then?" asked Roberta with blind supposition. Roberta had observed neither the previous dance nor its coupling, and Mariah, who did not know it, smiled in hesitation.

"Well, I am surprised by my feelings," Mariah paused and looked to her friend, "though I don't know how I could have missed it before…" said she half to herself. Roberta looked over, happy for a moment, then calmed herself.

"Now, I have news for you," said Roberta, "and I know you will be pleased. I have just been discussing our plans with Mrs Matlock, and what do you think she said?" Roberta asked, all excitement. "That she would discuss it directly with your uncle. How charming it will be for a summer spell in London. I don't think there is a fairer prospect." Roberta looked to her friend and paused. "But I see you have not yet caught your breath from dancing. He has quite worn you out." Mariah only smiled.

***

The next morning Mariah was awoken abruptly by the shouts and yells from women downstairs. She was sure one of the voices was Elizabeth, but could not place the other. She immediately rose and went downstairs. She found to her surprise that the other voice was Mrs Dunmead.

"Ladies, please," interjected Mariah, preventing another outburst from Mrs Dunmead. "It has barely struck nine." Mariah glared at them both. "Partridge Lodge may afford privacy for screaming hysterics, but unless you want the whole street to know your business, I suggest you moderate your voices before you mortify us all." To Mariah's disbelief, Elizabeth actually rolled her eyes and Mrs Dunmead sat down and turned away her head. After some gentle persuasion, and forced politeness, Mariah understood Elizabeth's cause for alarm. That her own mother, by her age and situation, had brought shame upon the family by her loose behaviour. Mrs Dunmead denied any wrongdoing and said that she was entitled to dance with whomever she chooses. Why should she not dance? Neither they nor she meant anything by it other than a little harmless fun. Elizabeth, seeing she would not change her mother's mind, quit the room, and Mrs Dunmead took her leave. Mariah, shaken by the hostilities, needed a good ten minutes' quiet reflection to be again calm.

She made herself ready for the day; after Edward's and Elizabeth's appearance at the ball the evening before, they were sure to get many bridal visits over the coming week. The first to call on them after breakfast was their Aunt and Uncle Matlock. Edward was pleased, Elizabeth was courteous and Mariah and Aunt Mary joined them in the drawing room. The Matlocks were prompt in their duties and civil in their enquiries. After which their Aunt Anna invited them all to dine with them the following evening. Before Elizabeth could object, as Edward was convinced his wife was about to turn them down, he warmly accepted the invitation for them all.

Mariah overheard raised voices later that morning above stairs before Edward adjourned to his study. After a half hour had passed away, she knocked on his door.

"What is it?" said he stiffly.

"It's only me," replied Mariah.

"Oh," said he, and he motioned for her to enter.

"There's a letter come from our cousins the Milcrofts."

"Ah. Thank you," said he, and shook his head. He then went on to hint at the depths of her misfortunes in Manchester before Mariah stopped him. She assured him that she understood perfectly as she had written and had a reply from Clare Milcroft; in short, she knew it all. Edward frowned and shook his head.

"I feel I must apologise also, dear Mariah, for the behaviour of my mother-in-law." Mariah was surprised and shook her head. "I have heard from more than one source that he is a favourite of yours, or at least you are a favourite of his…" Mariah laughed nervously and assured her brother that he was indeed mistaken. "Elizabeth was convinced as to its truth," said he surprised, "as was I… but it is of no matter if it not be the case." Mariah again assured her brother that was not the case at all. But she had not time to press her point as Mr and Mrs Marsh called on them that very moment.

After they had shared tea, Edward and Mr Marsh had a new scheme of business they wished to discuss while Mrs Marsh and Mariah decided to take a walk to the Forbury Gardens.

Roberta, convinced she would deeply miss her dear friend, especially now, spoke of her future felicity of seeing her in July. Mariah assured her friend that they would both be much too busy to notice the passing of four weeks. But Roberta protested.

"What shall I do, who shall I call on?" said she. Mariah laughed.

"But you forget our own neighbourhood, why Mrs Green is in need of volunteers for the annual garden party," replied Mariah. Roberta acknowledged at once that it had slipped her mind and fixed that she would speak with Mrs Green on Sunday.

At the Matlock's the following evening, the happy couple were toasted and prayed over. Both husband and wife played their parts with so many smiles and bows that their expected felicity was felt to be assured. Mrs Marsh did her utmost to include Mariah in their conversation, which of course frequently included Mr Harward. While Colonel Fanning and his wife wished Mariah and Aunt Mary a safe journey and handed Mariah a letter to give to the Miss Fannings.

Edward, free from entertaining his wife, on account of the happy enquiries of his aunt and uncle, was at liberty to observe Mr Harward and his sister, armed with his firm belief in her assertions the day before. Though he hardly knew why, for Mr Harward had all the appearance of a gentleman, with three thousand a year, and more handsome than some, Mariah resisted his charms. After dinner, Mrs Matlock found an opportunity to speak with her niece.

"Mr and Mrs Marsh told us of their going to London t'other day. And your uncle thought it such a good scheme that he has recommended to Edward and Eliza that we all go."

Mariah's heart sank—it was just as she feared: Roberta's eagerness had brought on a large party, and it was now certain her time would not be her own. Though she would never begrudge being joined by any of them by and by, the prospect of them all together was formidable. Mariah smiled in spite of herself.

"Really? I see, how charming that we should all be in Town together," returned Mariah.

"I knew you would be made happy by the news, especially as they are bringing a certain gentleman…hmm?"

"Oh, no, you mistake me, Aunt Anna," replied Mariah hastily. "I can assure you it had not entered my head… no…" continued she with all solemnity she could convey, "I was thinking of us all going to the London theatre."

"Well, yes there's that too…" replied Mrs Matlock happily surprised. She nodded a moment longer and considered from that time on that Mr Harward to be as fond of the theatre as her niece. "And perhaps, some new dresses," continued her aunt. Mariah agreed that new dresses certainly were a happy prospect.

***

Later the following day Mariah met with Lady Coburn in the gardens, who was quick to say that she was quite envious of her summer prospects. Sir Arthur's business would keep them in Reading the whole summer and she never liked to travel far without him. The theatre, and music to be experienced there, in her opinion, was second only to that of Vienna, which was a very great favourite of hers. And she added with the proviso, being of course, in Lady Coburn's understanding, of so little consequence to Mariah, that she would be in recurrent company of her favourite brother. Mariah could not but agree, though vainly hoped that the latter would not always be so little thought of to herself. The Lady's wording was so mild and her manner so gentle that Mariah could not determine if the connexion should be wholly given up that she paused her thoughts on the prospect for some time on her return journey.

Chapter Four

The Miss Fannings were overjoyed that Mariah and her aunt had finally arrived in London, as she had always been a favourite with them, and called on Mariah and Aunt Mary, at an early hour, the day after their arrival. The Miss Fannings were staying with their uncle and aunt, Mr and Mrs Dodd and their cousins, the latter whom Mariah had met lately in Reading. The Miss Fannings arrived with their aunt and uncle, but Mr Dodd waved them off at the door and said he'd be back for them in an hour.

***

Miss Marianne and Miss Margaret were all enthusiasm to share their exciting news and declared it at once: that they two had been specially invited to a second evening assembly with the full expectation of being joined by Mariah. The prospect was not unwelcome to Mariah, as it would likely be her last season in London and she agreed to it being a fixed engagement. The Miss Fannings then shared the particulars of their first evening assembly. The young ladies had made several new acquaintances, with little hints at some of them being very handsome indeed, they danced every dance and tried two cordials. At length, when their first raptures were over, Mariah presented the expected letter, followed by natural enquiries of health and happiness.

***

It was not unexpected that Aunt Mary declined the invitation to attend the evening assembly, favouring a little wool and crochet to the delights of a summer evening's outing. Mariah, however, in a new London gown purchased that week, arrived in a second carriage with the Miss Fannings and the eldest Miss Dodd, while the remaining Dodd family squeezed into the first.

The assembly was everything the young people wished, especially for the Miss Fannings, who spied two particular gentlemen, with whom they claimed an acquaintance. The said gentlemen were soon moving in their direction and after a brief presentation they were introduced as the Mr Littles and were dancing the next with the Miss Fannings, as a set. Mariah smiled and watched from afar.

After enquiries to Mrs Dodd, for Mr Dodd had taken a seat at the card tables, Mariah discovered that both gentlemen were of good family and situation, one a doctor and the other in the law, and were considered of an equal sphere. The Colonel and his family, though not wealthy, had put some little money aside for the marriage of his daughters, as his estate was entailed on his father's relations.

"It is a good match for Marianne, if she can get him. And Margaret too, I suppose," said Mrs Dodd. Mariah smiled.

"But Margaret is only sixteen," replied Mariah, "though of age, perhaps she is still a little young."

59

"Perhaps, but I am sure my brother will be pleased to know his daughters are being properly introduced into society. Young or not, a doctor and a lawyer from a good family is equal to their prospects, and I have no doubt will be well met with by him." Mariah immediately understood Mrs Dodd's undertaking for inviting her nieces to London and was only glad that she was not as young as they, lest she too fall prey to her schemes. "Pray, Miss Mariah, I have not yet heard you speak of any beau… I am sure there might be some hereabouts worthy of you. What about that gentleman over there…" Mariah almost laughed; a quick glance in his direction told her that he was already popular with the ladies.

"Thank you for your concern, Mrs Dodd, but really, I have no plans of matrimony for the present."

"Are you quite sure…? His name is Mr Rowley Price, he has a large estate in the north and six thousand a year… or was it seven…?" She paused and looked to Mariah for encouragement.

"Quite sure," replied Mariah, "besides, I believe he has enough attention already." Mrs Dodd could not but agree and laughed.

"No? No matter, no matter…" she nodded and continued. "You are a pretty girl… and with your fortune… well, I think you might do very well in the right circles, if you would but make your choice very soon?" Mariah made no answer and turned the conversation to Mrs Dodd's own children. It lamented Mrs Dodd to confess that she had not had much success with her eldest, Bridget either, at twenty-four with very little inclination for dance, and Mrs Dodd had all but given up on marrying her off, but her younger daughters Joany and Hannah were quite the opposite and she was in high hopes that Hannah, at least, would be married very soon.

***

One afternoon when Aunt Mary and Mariah had called on the Dodds, Bridget sought out Mariah's confidence.

"I am so glad you decided to come," said the eldest Miss Dodd, to Mariah. It had taken some, though very little persuasion for Mariah to agree to accompany the eldest Miss Dodd and the Miss Fannings to Vauxhall Gardens on account of a recommendation given by the Mr Littles. The Mr Littles had been very particular in their recommendation on account of some pretty wooded paths thereabouts, that one could get lost in them. It was enough to raise the hopes of adventure for the Miss Fannings, and the reservations of Mariah and Bridget.

The crowds were large and lively, the orchestras loud and the sun scorching. They waited by the promenade in hopes of seeing the Mr Littles; but to the disappointment of the Miss Fannings, neither man appeared. It took Mariah and Bridget some time to convince the young ladies that they had better enjoy the orchestras instead. Many pleasant hours were spent in this way, with only the occasional lament from one of the Miss Fannings at being deceived.

At length, Marianne suggested they take in one of the walks. Mariah was not immediately convinced as to it being a good plan. The Miss Fannings were sure to be as tired as herself, and it was getting late. She then suggested that they ought to be going. Marianne and Margaret, however, pleaded the opposite; as it was such a fine evening, it would be a terrific shame to waste it—surely one lane would do, instead of all the tour. Marianne solemnly promised Mariah and Miss Dodd that, if they took but one turn of the avenue she was sure to be content. Mariah hesitated, but at length agreed.

The crowds slowly dwindled as they made their way down the garden lane. The Miss Fannings walked on ahead while Mariah and Bridget walked along behind. When at the intersection she was approached by a gentleman and his companion.

"Miss Mariah, how delightful to see you," said Mr Tenby smilingly.

"Mr Tenby, it is, isn't it," replied Mariah with equal smiles. Mr Tenby then introduced his companion and cousin, Mr Probert, and Mariah presented Miss Dodd. When asked by Mr Tenby how they had enjoyed the gardens, both Mariah and Bridget spoke of how much they had enjoyed the orchestras.

"And did you dance?" asked Mr Probert grinning, "I saw several groups of people dancing." Bridget smiled but was silent, while Mariah confessed that neither of them had felt an inclination to dance, but that the Miss Fannings had enjoyed the exercise, as she pointed them out ahead. Upon looking in the direction, however, neither Marianne nor Margaret could be seen. Surprised, Bridget looked to Mariah.

"But where did they go?" asked Bridget. Both Mr Tenby and Mr Probert looked down the wooded lane and then back to Mariah and Bridget who were turning in every direction and then hurried down the lane to where the Miss Fannings had last been seen. Surprised by their haste, the two gentlemen hurried down the garden lane after Mariah and Bridget. Looking around again, Mariah could not immediately see them. She paused briefly while the others caught up, when she heard familiar giggles nearby. Upon further inspection,

Mariah spotted the two young ladies spying through the next copse of trees. Mariah was instantly relieved and immediately directed the others in her direction. The Miss Fannings, surprised at being caught prying, blushed scarlet and hastily ran back to the main avenue. Mariah gave stern looks to the young ladies but reserved her speeches of disappointment till Mr Tenby and his cousin had left.

On reaching Kennington Lane, Mr Tenby ordered the ladies a carriage, and Mariah thanked him again for his gentle kindness, while Bridget nodded in agreement and they departed.

They crossed the Regent Bridge before Mariah demanded, and dutifully received, an account of the behaviour of Margaret and Marianne. The Miss Fannings profusely apologised at once and pleaded with Mariah and their cousin in hopes that their reasons would lessen their guilt. Mariah and Bridget suspected some mischief was the case and decided to wait till their story was over before making an answer.

"Really, Mariah, we are very sorry for frightening you all, aren't we, Margaret?" said her elder sister. Margaret nodded. "But it's not our fault, not really. It was the fault of the Mr Littles." Their listeners were intrigued and listened to the whole confession in silence. Margaret had spied one of the Mr Littles first; he was walking by a little way off, in another lane. Their interest caught, they could not help but get nearer. But on doing so they felt such agonies on their discovery; because he was not with his brother but two young ladies.

Marianne paused and looked to Mariah and Bridget appealingly. "So you see, we had to get closer." They had then overheard them talking as sweetly as they had done to their own selves, with the same stories and nonsense.

"It sounded so ridiculous hearing it a second time," added Margaret, trying not to smile, "we simply had to follow them."

Mariah smirked and her displeasure instantly went away; she tried very hard not to smile and agreed that she probably would have done the same. Bridget smiled also and with a shake of her head admitted that it is that way with some people, and if she was entirely honest, she never liked them anyway. Mariah decided to say no more about it if the Miss Fannings had learned by it, which they said they had.

Mariah and Aunt Mary were another week in London before Mr Tenby called on them with an invitation to one of his uncle's card parties. The card was linen, the print was an elegant blue and in the corner was the Tenby family crest. Mr Tenby then added that, of course, the Miss Fannings and Miss Dodd were also most welcome. Mariah felt this most kind and told him so at once, and that she would convey their invitation to them on the morrow, as Aunt Mary and herself were for the museum this very hour.

"But that is exactly where my cousin and I are going," said he. Mariah was happily surprised. "You recommended it so highly, I knew it must be done."

"And is Mr Probert with you this very moment?" asked Mariah, astonished.

"He is! He's just waiting outside in the carriage."

The ladies then joined Mr Tenby and Mr Probert on a tour of the museum. Aunt Mary spoke of her amazement and delight of the marble sculptures. After they had viewed the second gallery of marble artefacts, Aunt Mary continued to the early century vases, which surpassed even Mariah's admiration. Aunt Mary, however, found an avid listener and enthusiastic companion in Mr Probert, while Mariah directed Mr Tenby toward the curiosities from the South Seas.

When Mariah and Aunt Mary were alone that evening, Aunt Mary enquired after the curiosities Mariah had surveyed. Mariah only said she found them interesting; Aunt Mary smiled.

"I see, I have no doubt of course that your companion was far more fascinating than mine." Mariah blushed a little.

"I thought his interest was equal to your own?" replied Mariah.

"He was surely eager to impart his knowledge."

"Yes, he is, isn't he?" Mariah nodded.

"Yes, his conversation is certainly voluble."

***

The following day Mariah conveyed the invitation to the Miss Fannings and Miss Dodd.

"Oh, that is thoughtful…" said Margaret feebly.

"Oh no! We cannot go, next Tuesday you say? No, no," added Marianne.

"Why ever not?" enquired Mrs Dodd, eager to have her daughter and nieces mix with higher society.

"It sounds awfully dull, and there is an evening assembly that night and we are expected!" replied Marianne defiantly.

"Indeed we are!" added Margaret.

"Surely Mr…. what was his name?" began Mrs Dodd.

"Granger…" supplied Margaret.

"Yes, yes! I am sure he will do very well without you for one evening. You would be better off with Mariah at the

Tenby's than young men with little to recommend them other than their fine clothes and academic achievements."

"But, Aunt Deirdre, we promised… Let Bridget go, she can tell us all about it," pleaded Margaret.

"I doubt that," murmured Marianne to her sister, "for there will be nothing to tell. We will have more to report than she." The Miss Fannings giggled, Mrs Dodd shook her head and Mariah smiled.

Aunt Mary was, however, most relieved on two counts, the first being that, as Miss Dodd was to accompany Mariah, she could remain comfortably at home and the second was that Mr Probert would have to find another listener for his voluble speeches.

***

On their way home from Hans Place after a delightful and grand evening, Mariah and Bridget, of course, discussed the evening's events.

"By the by, Bridget, I must thank you for your services to me." Mariah smiled.

"How so?" asked Bridget.

"I am in your debt." Mariah continued. Bridget looked puzzled. "You listened to Mr Probert so patiently and occupied his attentions so diligently, he quite forgot his cousin."

"Oh," Bridget smiled. "No, you are mistaken." It was now Mariah's turn to be confused.

"Surely not…" replied Mariah, surprised. Bridget smiled.

"From our first meeting in Vauxhall Gardens, I have esteemed his company; he was so very kind to my cousins and myself that day. I cannot forget his kindness."

"They were never really in danger, you know," replied Mariah.

"But they might have been," added Bridget hastily, "there really was no knowing what could have happened."

"Well, mind how you go, esteem is all very well, but it would not do to be encouraging." Bridget looked dismayed, then Mariah added: "Unless that is your intention?"

"I know you think him a little verbose, but really he is not so very dull…" replied Bridget, "and at length, he is in want of an answer." Mariah smiled.

"And could you give one?"

"Oh yes, well, some of the time…" She paused, then added, "I know too, he is a little older, but age has its benefits also." Mariah nodded slowly. "He is to join us for a walk tomorrow."

"Well, I hope it is a fine day for you all." Bridget agreed and hoped that it would be also.

Chapter Five

The following week, despite Elizabeth's hopes for lodgings at Cavendish Square, Edward and his wife joined Mariah and Aunt Mary at High Holborn Street, and, not counting her minute inspection of the entire apartment, it was done so with very little fuss.

Mrs Matlock having previously spoken to her husband of Mariah's desire to attend the theatre together, he called on them the day after their arrival to tell them that a box had been secured for the following evening. Elizabeth listened intently; Edward thought it a good plan and Aunt Mary, like Mariah, received the news with pleasure. Mr Matlock, however, was by no means finished telling all and with little more than a brief pause continued enthusiastically.

"I have just received a note this very hour that the Colonel and Mrs Fanning shall be joining us… and," said he, turning to face Mariah, "with them will be Mr and Mrs Marsh and… a Mr Harward." He smiled broadly, believing he had done his niece a good turn and all eyes turned toward her. Mariah immediately felt the awkwardness of their misconception; it was, however, a most unfortunate time to blush, as it only added to their mistaken confidence in her admiration of him. She struggled for speech to say anything to change their understanding, but at every turn of her mind, her unspoken words seemed the feeble mewing protests of a bashful lover. At length, she was grateful for the timing of her aunt, who unexpectedly changed the conversation to that of the new plays to be seen in London.

That evening, after prayerful and reflective considerations, Mariah measured her admiration of Mr Harward against that of Mr Tenby; she felt some guilt for her initial encouragement, as now she had not even once considered Mr Harward from their last meeting, till now. She had spent many happy weeks in London in the company of others. She could safely say she justly valued him without any fervent admiration of his character or person. It disturbed her greatly then that her acquaintances, in general, were always trying to bring about her happiness. How pitiable her situation; for though she had denied her admiration for him many times over, she had not been believed. She felt it even more so when she was purposefully sat by Mr Harward the following evening at the theatre. She smiled briefly and dared not sigh lest he hear her disappointment; it would not do to encourage conversation, nor confidences with someone with whom she was trying to dissuade from her whole acquaintance.

"I am determined," said Mr Harward quietly to her, when they were seated, "to secure your affections..." He paused, then added quieter still, "I've heard it said 'Opposition is true friendship', but I say it is true fancy..." Mariah's face reddened; she absolutely had to make her objections known now, but she had barely uttered a syllable of her first reproof when they were hushed by the others in the box; because just at that moment, the performance began.

***

"Now, my dear one," said Mrs Marsh to Mariah when they were next together. "I cannot begin to tell you how frequently Mr Harward spoke of you since you went to London. It really has been frightfully long since I saw you last, and Mrs Green was constant in her desire of my assistance for the annual garden party; I am quite worn out! But enough of that. You must tell me how you've managed these many weeks alone in London. Though I am sure you will tell me that you have borne it all without so much as a frown, but of course, I shan't believe you." Mariah smiled at her friend and hesitated for an answer.

"Well, of course, I have missed you, but I have had company." Roberta was all attention.

"Anybody we know?" asked Mrs Marsh. Mariah explained how she had spent time with the Colonel's daughters and their cousin's family; she hesitated again, before mentioning Mr Tenby and his cousin. "Oh yes, well, I'm not sure Lady Coburn would like that. Though I am sure there is no harm in being acquainted, unlike Mr Harward of course, whose current situation at present is not as wealthy as some, I grant you… but then when his father dies, he'll inherit everything. And that is a tidy sum. Though I have it on good authority that his allowance, at present, is considerable." Mariah made no answer. "Any young lady, like yourself, would be foolish indeed to throw away his affections. He is a good man, Mariah, well worthy of you, my dear one." Mariah raised her eyebrows. "Indeed, he is, I know your brother thinks so, as do the Matlocks; do you really think I would match my intimate friend with anyone unworthy of you? Though I can see he has not won you over just yet, but I will trust you will see his good qualities by and by."

Mariah bore it all with patience and humility. It was true, she could not understand her reluctance to Mr Harward's advances, other than to say they had been too liberally applied and if she were not careful, she may yet have no other choice. It seemed apparent and unfortunate that these opinions and feelings could not be expressed by any means to her family and friends from Reading, on account of their partiality for him. But she did, however, know a friend who understood these feelings all too well.

That friend was Miss Bridget, who was in want of a companion to accept an invitation from Mr Probert and another friend, to Ranelagh Gardens for reasons that her brother was far too young to appreciate the expense, and her sisters and cousins were all of them no way inclined either by venue or company. It was Miss Dodd who mentioned it first, on account of her impression being that her unspoken and unacknowledged admiration lay another way. Mariah smiled and sighed with relief.

"I cannot begin to tell you how it relieves me to hear you speak so. Even my friends seem determined that I should marry him as soon as may be. Though I have steadily denied any feelings of the kind. But as I am sure you know all too well, our hearts' desires are not often considered, let alone made truth." Bridget acknowledged Mariah's solemn words wholeheartedly. "At twenty-seven, I have managed to elude them all... till now."

"I admire you, your determination, and it gives me courage. And I too, who have a mother that is in haste, but I do believe that not dancing has been my saving grace." Mariah laughed with Bridget.

"It seems you are right, dancing may have been my downfall…" Mariah paused and looked to the two gentlemen a little way off. "But you must tell me, Bridget, since we last spoke, how oft have you met?"

Bridget could not help but smile and acknowledged that they had been in company thrice, twice intentionally but a third time was wholly unexpected through a common acquaintance. Then she added, "He is a good match for me, I think; he is attentive to me, tempered and so generous. Despite first impressions, we really do have similar interest and taste in both history and music."

Mariah smiled and agreed that it indeed sounded promising.

"And when are you next to see Mr Tenby?" asked Bridget.

"I hardly know," confessed Mariah. "It is all too awkward at present. And as Mrs Marsh said the other day, neither his uncle nor his sister, Lady Coburn, has endorsed the connexion."

"But surely you will not resign yourself to this Mr Harward?"

"No, no indeed…" Mariah shook her head.

"Though I know nothing of him, is he very bad, do you think?"

"I don't know," admitted Mariah. "I can't explain it, his flattery, though profusely spoken and acted… it somehow feels insincere to me. As if he is determined to persuade his own heart as well as mine of his affections."

"Well, I must confess, by your own words, I do agree there does appear to seem to be some urgency in the case. Do you have grounds to doubt your own reasoning? … As a friend I would caution you to trust your own feelings, you must allow your own judgement to guide you. If you doubt his sincerity, and you find his character disreputable…" Bridget paused, then added, "Hmm, and do you know his reasons for marriage?" Mariah shook her head. "Perhaps for reasons of money, does he have debts? Will he come into money upon his marriage?"

"Such as a gamester? Oh, if only it were that easy, Edward would never consent to a connexion with a gamester. Especially after my uncle's profligate lifestyle. No, sadly, he has all the appearance of a gentleman."

On returning from the gardens Mariah was met with Elizabeth, who took it upon herself to immediately share the good news of their connexions with Mariah. Edward and Elizabeth had been invited to a dinner at Hans Place. But before Elizabeth could say any more, Edward, who had been listening to the whole of his wife's speech, added that Mariah too was expressly invited. When Edward quit the room, Elizabeth could not help but add that Mariah needn't smile so much as Mr Harward had not been invited and it was unlikely she would have been invited at all had it not been for Edward's connexions. Elizabeth narrowed her eyes and lowered her voice for Mariah's hearing only; that she was sure any such gentleman who attended a dinner at Hans Place was well out of Mariah's influence. Mariah's smile faltered, but she made no answer and sat in the dim parlour for a quarter hour unobserved by anyone else except her dear Aunt Mary.

"It amuses and saddens me that souls can be built up and destroyed so quickly by the rapid tongues of fools without a care as to feelings, hopes or dreams. But it would make fools of us all if wounded we let it be the final say." Mariah kissed her Aunt Mary and thanked her for her kind words.

Mariah, after another quarter hour's reflection, led herself to believe that an invite to Hans Place, let alone a dinner, was through her own particular connexion with the Tenbys in both Reading and London. She was, however, unsure of Elizabeth's reasons for malice; was it purely out of spite or did she really know of her partiality for Frederick's company and wish to put her off? At length, she forgot about Elizabeth's attempts to upset her and turned her attentions to something much more frivolous, of whether she should wear her new yellow gown or the white.

At the dinner, Mariah was both delighted and pleased to see both Mr Probert and Miss Bridget were guests at the dinner also; more too was her pleasure as she was seated diagonally from Miss Dodd and away from Elizabeth. She would pleasantly avoid any conversation with her, as there were twelve to dine.

Sir Niels Tenby, Frederick's uncle, a fashionable man of older tastes and splendour, ensured his guests were seated with the opposing gender, except for his nephew, like himself, seated at Carver.

He very much disliked not knowing what people were about and regarded himself as an attentive uncle and host, to whatever his niece and nephew may require; even acting on their behalf, if he thought it for the best.

Although the newlyweds were seated together, betwixt them were people with whom Mariah was familiar, but had only met in passing at card parties. But she need not have worried, however, for Elizabeth spent the better part of the evening in wonderment of both the host and his lavish style.

Sir Niels's self-indulgences extended far beyond his love of French Claret and playing high at cards; his table was expertly filled with meats, game and pies, two of which were replaced before the dishes were removed. Mariah, not unaccustomed to grand tables, saw Elizabeth's wonder with silent amusement.

***

When the gentleman again joined the ladies for tea, some of the ladies, Mariah included, were invited to play. Elizabeth, however, with no talent for music, complimented the host with steady adulation on the arrangement of his table, the size of his rooms, and for a short while, drew the attention of the host.

Bridget confessed that she did not play half as well as Mariah, but would happily sing along. Their performance was admired and applauded, especially by two particular gentlemen. Sir Niels, however, gave a dutiful applause and looked in Mariah's direction with a studied air. Mariah smiled politely and stood up to allow one of the other ladies to play and sing.

Over the next few days, Mariah's attentions were directed and decided by Edward's engagements, Elizabeth's measures and Mrs Marsh's schemes. Three days in Mr Harward's company delighted everyone except herself. Mariah, however, found unexpected solace in the company of the Miss Fannings, who spoke endlessly of some new acquaintance, evening assemblies, and dancing; they helped her forget what she could not, at present, bring herself to accept. It was generally believed by some of her acquaintance that she was stalling for reasons they assumed, rather than knew, and did not take the time to ask. Some, like her brother, and her Aunt and Uncle Matlock thought her a rational creature, enjoying one final season in London, and were sure that she would commit to his advances on returning home to Reading. But Elizabeth saw it all through her own vexation that Mariah had acted by design to be a continued burden on her brother's finances, and Elizabeth's nerves.

The day before Edward, Elizabeth and all those that had lately joined them from Reading were to leave London, Elizabeth found herself alone with Mariah.

"Now, let me give you a little hint of my feelings. For I do believe you have been quite favoured during our stay. Though I doubt it will continue once we leave, no one will want your society, my dear, so I am sure, you will have very little expense, as you will have nothing to do. Of course, no one begrudges you little pleasures, but really I do think, at your age, you have seen and done it all before." Elizabeth paused and nodded, Mariah made no answer and then with a slow drawing of breath through her nose, Elizabeth continued. "Whatever your pretence for delay, I assure you, when you return to us, I expect Mr Harward's offer to be taken seriously, or else you can be assured of my disapproval, which I shall, of course, bring to Edward's attention. Mr Harward's affections can be put off indefinitely, but a brother's security cannot." Elizabeth smiled but did not look at Mariah. "But I trust you will give in to him when you are back in Reading. It is expected, and I know he intended to make you an offer while in London, but it does not seem he has had the chance because you have insisted on rejecting a respectable man. I just thought you should know, and ensure we understand each other."

Elizabeth then quit the room, and Mariah, overcome with feelings, sought a quiet corner in the library.

Mariah felt the truth of Elizabeth's words in the days after their departure. The Miss Fannings, who had been frequent in their attentions, had returned with their mother and father to Reading. Mr Tenby had not called on her and it had been a fortnight since their last meeting. Miss Dodd, likewise, was otherwise engaged, as relatives of Mr Probert were in Town and he, of course, desired her to make their acquaintance.

It surprised her all the more then that someone should call on them so early. To her utter amazement, it was Sir Niels Tenby who crossed the vestibule in quick step and was announced in the drawing room. She immediately put down her book and greeted him with courtesy. Mariah's awkwardness increased as he did not immediately speak but instead surveyed the room. She could not think of his reasons for calling, as she was sure he understood Edward to have left on Tuesday.

"Shall I order tea, Sir Niels, it is a little early, but..." began Mariah; her guest appeared to be in anxieties of his speech. Sir Niels shook his head and looked out the window at the passing carriages. Mariah immediately understood that this regarded her connexion with his nephew, and she sat down and with a deep breath prepared her mind to receive it.

He spoke with regret of Mariah not having heard from Frederick this fortnight passed. "I know," said he, "because I intercepted the letter. I do not want you to be misled."

"Oh," was her only reply.

He cleared his throat and without raising his voice spoke with increasing outrage of his disappointment at not being shown the same courtesy, that he had been misled by the connexion and that she, Mariah, ought to be ashamed of herself. "A respectable young lady ought not… is not, capable of duplicity and dishonesty." And by his estimation, she was, therefore, not a respectable young lady, and could not claim any part of propriety or respectability for herself. Sir Niels required no answer and surely Mariah had none to give; her shock and distress at being addressed in such a way unsettled her exceedingly.

After a brief pause he continued on to say that as he was sure she was now of his understanding, it would not come as a surprise that he would never allow his nephew to be united in marriage with anyone so unfeeling. Mariah was surprised by his continued addresses; she expected disapproval of a nearer connexion, but not to be accused of impropriety or of destroying his nephew's character and good name. She did not hear the rest of his speech, nor see him leave, only the closing of the front door.

It was a good many hours' silence that followed these words; not even the servants disturbed her solitude. Yet, by the time Aunt Mary returned that evening, she was recovered enough to conceal the whole ordeal.

Chapter Six

Miss Dodd did not forget her new friend and learned, after perceiving Mariah's affected composure, and with earnest encouragement, of the uncle's unexpected visit. Mariah's mortification, however, would never allow her to disclose the whole of the conversation, other than to say she had been accused of impropriety. On hearing Mariah's brief confession, Bridget could not account for his reasoning, for Mariah and her family were highly respected in Reading and well regarded by all her family; Mariah in despair believed she deserved it all.

Bridget supposed that there must be some mistake. Mariah insisted it was so and more too, acknowledged it all to be her own fault, that she was divided from Mr Tenby forever, for she had not first sought approval for the connexion; they were, after all, superior to her own family.

"To accuse you of impropriety, though," added Bridget; it seemed to her a gross miscarriage of supposition and feeling. Mariah shook her head, for the rich will speak as they choose; as they are accustomed. Bridget could not disagree more wholeheartedly and added with such conviction that the difference was not all that much and certainly it was the Tenbys who had lost a great treasure and more so, Bridget was convinced, that anyone who knew Mariah would never accept this estimation of her character. Mariah smiled briefly but lamented that to all this she must add another disgrace! Mariah did not know how she would ever face Lady Coburn again; if not at present, she was sure that Lady Coburn would soon be acquainted with all.

Her feelings, though well concealed, did not go unnoticed by her aunt. Miss Dodd, also without expectation, saw no real improvement in Mariah's solemness for several days and was on the lookout for a project by way of distraction. Mr Probert suggested it first, though he had no knowledge of Sir Niels's speech, nor Mariah's feelings. But he knew of Frederick being called away and to give both Miss Dodd and Miss Mariah occupation as to distract the latter at least from his absence, he devised a small plan. But before Bridget had opportunity to convey the new project to her friend, Mariah announced to Aunt Mary and Miss Dodd that she wished to return home early.

Mariah declared her reasons at once, before objections were made; that she was tired of London society, for there was nothing to do, and her thinking had been the work of several days' consideration. Her final reason, though she would not share it outside her own thoughts, was decided when she was made acquainted with the news that Mr Tenby had been seen about Town with a Miss Harper of Fingen Park in Hampshire, worth forty thousand pounds.

To Bridget's relief and Mariah's disappointment, it was Aunt Mary that prevented an early escape, as she had plans for another fortnight. Mariah, who could never disappoint her aunt, agreed to stay, at least till the end of a fortnight, but she would write to Edward all the same for a speedy assurance of their London accounts.

Secured of Mariah's continued company, Bridget immediately spoke of Mr Probert's idea for a picnic at Sydenham Hill, that it had been left to Bridget to arrange and that she was desperately in need of assistance; that is to say Mariah's assistance. Mariah accepted with pleasure, and as both Miss Dodd and Mr Probert had hoped, it was distraction enough to see Mariah was again made contented.

Despite the early anxieties of the scheme, the arrangements were progressing well, the invitations were sent, the repast decided and both Mr Dodd and Mr Probert were to provide carriages and horses, but Mariah began to become more troubled. Though she would not, on this occasion, share her troubles with Bridget, she did confess them to her Aunt Mary, for Edward had not replied, their bills had not been discharged, and they could not depart Tuesday next as planned.

By the day of the picnic, still, no word had been received from Edward, though now two letters had been sent. Neither she nor Aunt Mary could comprehend the mystery. Aunt Mary too had written to Edward and had no reply. She did, however, begin to suspect some other reason for the delay and encouraged Mariah to write instead to her Aunt and Uncle Matlock for explanations.

The day was pleasant, and Sydenham Hill and the view of the Great North Wood was as picturesque as promised. The younger Miss Dodds and Mr Probert's sister took out paper and pencils to sketch the beauty before them, while Aunt Mary and Mrs Dodd admired the view and spoke of days gone by when they used to paint in water colours just so.

The real reason for the picnic, however, was entirely different, though not wholly unexpected. Mr Probert announced to all, in his usual verbose way, that today was a very important day, as he had particularly sought an audience with Mr Dodd earlier that morning, on a topic that was very near to him and would determine him to be the happiest of men. The young ladies, having heard the beginning of his speech, put down their tools at once and turned to face him, as such a beginning surely meant something grand. Bridget could barely contain her happiness and Mr Probert continued. And so, having been successful in his earnest request to both the father and the daughter, they should all congratulate them directly, as he and Miss Dodd were to be married. Mrs Dodd was in raptures at finally having a daughter married and the sisters happily expressed their delight.

In the quiet of the afternoon, as many of the guests had taken a walk in the Great North Wood, Mariah expressed her joyful delight for them both and wished them both very happy.

"Oh Mariah, I am so happy. I once recall you saying that you were indebted to me for having distracted him so, but really, it is I who am indebted to you. And to think that you almost did not come that day in the gardens is unthinkable now." Mariah grinned and nodded. "And I do hope to see you soon as happy as I, though at present it might seem unlikely. I am sure it will come right in the end." Mariah smiled; she could not bear to hope just now, as it seemed improbable at best and at worst, it would not do to despair.

Unlike her previous correspondence to Edward, her Uncle John replied directly with surprising news as to make Aunt Mary certain of her suspicions.

My Dear Niece,

I hope this letter finds you and dear Aunt Mary well and enjoying your summer in London. We are all quite recovered from our journey; we are all well. The Miss Fannings have called on us twice with Mrs Fanning to hear news of your return, for you are dearly missed! They tell us the most amazing stories of gardens, dinners and of a Mr Tenby—we think there must be some misunderstanding in the case, but they were most insistent. Although we have urged them to say no more about it to anyone else.

But your next point, dear Mariah, is rather disturbing and puzzling to us and we cannot account for it at all, other than to find it most strange indeed. Be not alarmed, dear Niece, for your brother and Elizabeth are quite well, they dined with us last week! You may be astonished to know, they have been home this past month, only Monday last has business taken Edward away. Had I known sooner, I most definitely would have spoken with him then, but I will do so directly when he comes. And now he is to be gone a half month!

For now, I will not have you nor your aunt in unnecessary anxieties and I must insist that you send me the list of creditors forthwith and I will satisfy them directly. I know what you might say, but on this point, I must insist and expect a reply, with the asked for list, by the end of the week.

Your aunt and I wish you safe travels home,

Regards

Yours, Uncle John.

"It is a wonder to me that she would attempt it," said Aunt Mary after Mariah had read her the letter, "Edward will be most displeased, yet I am certain that she has done it." Mariah looked confused.

"You don't believe they have been lost in the mail then?" asked Mariah. Aunt Mary laughed.

"No!" replied Aunt Mary. "No, though she will deny any knowledge, I am convinced the servants will know better."

But Mariah was at a loss to understand. "I don't understand how anyone could be so cruel, Aunt. I really cannot understand such malice."

"Of course not, my dear, you have a good heart and always try to do your best for others. But not everyone is the same. And I believe that your brother's wife, whose meanness we are yet to fully comprehend, is the very opposite, for it is more than avariciousness, it is a desire to afflict most cruelly. It is what I glimpsed when we were first acquainted, but it took me several weeks to know for sure."

"But are you quite sure, Aunt? I am not sure she really is as vicious as all that? I do hope you are wrong, I know she is foolish and not very kind, but surely that is a step too far. Surely no one can be that unkind."

"Hmmph! Money and influence are vast instigators and you'd be well advised to take heed," replied her aunt.

Mariah believed and hoped that her aunt had overestimated Elizabeth's wants and desires and was sure some misunderstanding was at play.

Unbeknownst to those of Reading, and entirely hidden from Elizabeth, there was one great advantage of being delayed long in London. It was their growing acquaintance with the Dodds and Mr Probert, who felt it a genuine advantage to their company, for both Mariah and Aunt Mary were highly esteemed and much respected and in turn, invited to and attended the wedding of the eldest Miss Dodd and Mr Probert.

Mariah, who had not been in company with Mr Tenby since Edward's leaving London, expected, with no small amount of anxiety, his presence at the wedding of his cousin and friend and more too that of his uncle. She even, on more than one occasion, doubted her right to be there, but when Bridget heard of this, she immediately asserted her persuasions. That both Mr Probert and herself thought the world of Mariah as it was she who brought them together; in their view, both Mariah and Mr Tenby had more of an entitlement than favour, priority more than due. And to make the event more agreeable to Mariah, spoke of their regret as Sir Niels was unable to make an appearance. Mariah was relieved by this news and agreed that both she and Aunt Mary would happily attend.

Mariah's only hesitation now was Mr Tenby's newest connexion, possibly even now his betrothed. She hoped that there would be little to say, and if she kept herself occupied in the attentions of others, they would scarcely have opportunity to speak. It was no small surprise then that the prosperous Miss Harper was not one of the guests and Mariah supposed the wedding party had been kept small. She imagined also, more than once, that Mr Frederick Tenby would wish to avoid an audience with herself also after his uncle's speeches.

She took great care to attend to her aunt whether by seating or in another small way or under the pretence of captivation, and lent herself to various conversations, till unexpectedly she found herself alone. She looked around in earnest for some occupation, but she was not swift enough, for at that moment Mr Tenby, who had patiently waited for an opportunity, approached.

"You have been quite attentive to the needs of others, why don't you take a little wine and come sit by me. I know it to be several weeks since we last met, but you ought to forgive me as it has not been my own doing. Unfortunately, I am at my uncle's bidding at times, and that takes me away, but come, we have not spoken for some time. Tell me, what you have been doing, Mr Probert has told me of his own account of dinners, gardens and picnics, but I would prefer your own view? One can hardly take seriously the word of a man in love. He will add fancies and flourishes at will, say nothing of actual accounts and speak of everything as the best that ever was."

Mariah could not help but grin. "I cannot contradict you at all, sir."

"How so?" asked he.

"While you have had the advantage of the groom's perception, I have had the bride's, and I am sure the accounts are not so dissimilar as to not make it a dull repetition. But of my account, I own it will be very plain; I am not sure you could bear such tedium." Mr Tenby laughed and denied her claims of dullness, and assured her that he was of the belief that he would never consider her words to be tedious. It was his own view that her account would be so similar to his own experience had he been one of the party, and he gently encouraged her all the more. Mariah could scarcely refuse such a kind request; she recounted it all, with due care as to leave out his uncle's visit. "There now," said he, "I was so sure that your own ideas would be comparable to my own view, I am not at all disappointed. Though I am sorry I was not there that day at Ranelagh Gardens, it truly sounds a wonder, even your own account was something to be admired. I am quite envious."

On later reflection, Mariah was surprised by his interest and attention to herself. Mariah and indeed a weaker woman could be easily led to believe he was not interested in Miss Harper at all, but that would never do as she knew it to be false. The one thing she had feared above all, for she was convinced it was more than her spirits could bear, was his speeches on Miss Harper, and he had not done it, not even hinted. She began to think of him more highly than before and hoped that Miss Harper would endeavour to deserve him.

Mr Probert and his bride departed for their wedding tour the following day, on their way south and would return via Reading before settling in—not twenty miles from Mariah.

Chapter Seven

Mariah and Aunt Mary longed to be home soon after the wedding. The anticipated home comforts of quietude and familiarity were looked for, but not received by either of them. Upon arrival, Elizabeth did not greet them nor welcome them home and before they had tea in the downstairs parlour, they were informed by a maid, not familiar to them, that their things had been taken to their room on the ground floor. Aunt Mary stared at the young maid in astonishment.

"I beg your pardon, I am sure I have misheard you, I thought you said my room… is on the ground floor."

"Yes Madam, that's right."

Both Mariah and Aunt Mary put down their cups and saucers immediately and followed the maid to their room. The rooms on the ground floor had always been a little neglected due to their lack of use, and although they had been tidied, the walls and furnishings looked worn and old.

Mariah's astonishment overwhelmed her for several moments, but Aunt Mary's good sense was inflamed with a fiery disgust! She turned back to the parlour and informed the servant that she desired an immediate audience with Elizabeth. It was some time before Elizabeth joined them in the parlour and without taking a seat she apologised for her delay, as she was entertaining guests in the upstairs parlour.

"Oh, you must excuse me, has it been an hour already?" said Elizabeth in her usual trim and dainty voice. "I am so very busy, so many things to arrange, I haven't begun to look into the refurbishment of the rooms on the ground floor, you must see that there are other rooms in the terrace that desperately need my attention." She paused and Aunt Mary was about to speak her mind when Elizabeth began again. "Oh, and do not worry as I have made sure our honoured and noble guests are quite well looked after, though several new carpets were purchased, and some new wallpaper, and such a collection of old things… I knew it all had to be removed, I was going to burn them, of course, but lo… the footman convinced me to put them aside till later, so, I've had them taken to the attic."

"Such confidence while the Master is away? Though I can hardly say I am surprised," began Aunt Mary, but Elizabeth interjected.

"Oh indeed, I did think you would feel much more at home at Grimstead Cottage, which has just become vacant. Old Mr Pottage died last week. But it is not quite ready for new tenants." Elizabeth shook her head at their shocked faces. "Oh my dears, you see, you've become too accustomed to our fortunate ways, and I feel it is not good to raise your expectations to undue distinction. But it was my mother that convinced me to let you stay… at least until Edward returns." She smiled at them both and checked the time, and spoke again of her noble guests from Ramsgate, and that as a fine meal had only been prepared for the six of them, she would ask the kitchen to send some broth and bread to their room.

"Oh by the by," added Elizabeth before quitting the room, "your letters came yesterday, of course, I can forward them to him in Oxford if you think it ought to be done, but as you were to arrive today, I thought it best to ask you before it was done. I dare say you will have new things to write to him about now." Elizabeth smiled sweetly.

"How odd that letters posted four weeks hence arrive the very day before our arrival. It is such a coincidence it is beyond belief," said Aunt Mary disapprovingly.

"Indeed, four weeks is considerable; how very shocking of the Royal Mail! I did not know they were so very bad in these parts. Though sometimes, if the direction is poorly written, it does hinder the delivery of the letters."

"And yet the direction was perfectly formed; I am particular," replied Aunt Mary.

"But of course you are." Elizabeth smiled. "So, it must be the fault of the service, they do hire the most unskilled lowly people these days..." and with nothing more to say on the subject, Elizabeth quit the room.

A quarter hour later when Mariah and her aunt had returned to the parlour, Mrs Dunmead happened upon them. She was gracious in her address but soon turned the conversation to that of her eldest daughter's plans; even Elizabeth's own mother had not escaped unscathed by her cruelty and that Elizabeth had confessed to her mother of hopes that Mariah and Aunt Mary would be gone by Christmas but added, she hoped, very much hoped for her own sanity's sake, that this was not the case.

Though on first determination, Aunt Mary in much umbrage penned a terse letter to Edward on the recent follies of his wife, she did not, however, immediately give it over to be dispatched. After recent events, she mistrusted any confidentiality from Elizabeth and doubted its reaching Edward at all.

It was fortunate, then, that Mariah and Aunt Mary were made happy by news the following day, for Edward's business had been completed sooner than expected and he was to return by the end of the week.

After three days alone and without additional company, Mariah began to wonder why her friends had not called on her; perhaps, thought she, they did not know she had returned. She intended to call on her aunt and uncle that morning and enquired after the carriage but was surprised to find the footman was unobliging and regrettably advised her that his mistress had given strict instructions as to its use for the guests. Mariah understood that though he would have gladly assisted her, Elizabeth was trying her best to upset her. Aunt Mary, who had felt a little poorly since their return to Reading, was in no condition to walk three and a quarter miles to the Matlock's, and so Mariah was forced to hire a carriage to take them thither.

They received a very warm welcome at the Matlock's and after a little encouragement and discussion about Elizabeth and their troubles, they kindly, but firmly, insisted Mariah and Aunt Mary dine with them that day. The ladies readily accepted, for it had been several days that they had eaten little more than bread and broth. Upon hearing this Mariah's uncle was greatly alarmed and made up his mind to speak with Edward to remedy the evil immediately. He had believed the problem with the post, like Mariah, to be due to some misunderstanding, but this duplicity was far beyond anything he had ever expected.

Mariah added a little while later that neither Mrs Marsh nor any of her other friends had called on them, but here Mrs Matlock added that Mrs Marsh had been turned away when she enquired after Mariah. Aunt Mary was neither surprised nor shocked by this news and resisted the urge to assert that Elizabeth had done exactly as she suspected several weeks before; unlike Mariah, who was most astonished.

While Aunt Mary remained at home, Mariah was grateful for the short walk to Minster Street to call on Mrs Marsh.

"Oh, I have been so worried," cried Mrs March, "I was sure that something had happened to you and your aunt, I said so to Mr M, did I not, Mr M?" she continued in earnest. Mr Marsh nodded from behind his book. "And to think your brother's wife would not give me a hint of the delay; instead she wished me gone! Sent the new maid to dismiss me without so much as a greeting. Did she not, Mr M?"

"Yes, darling Roberta. As 'bout as most discourteous as you can get, I'd say," added Mr Marsh before returning to his book. Mrs Marsh then repeated her own encounter with the Miss Fannings at the Matlock's and her amusement at the wild tales told of their adventures in London, before referring to her husband to assure Mariah as to its truth. At this Mr Marsh respectfully excused himself and quit the room; Mariah supposed, with some amusement, that he may have wished to read his book in peace. Roberta then, to Mariah's disappointment, returned to her favourite subject, Mr Harward.

"Oh, but you must come, my dear one. He has asked after you most steadily, and I know he will be thrilled to see you again," pleaded Roberta, who knew of Mr Harward's plans for a little ball at Partridge Lodge. "He even has three hirelings from London, though I know they are here for another reason. Which reminds me, you must call on Lady Coburn, she has the most exciting news."

Mariah was surprised by the turn of the conversation and scarcely managed a reply. "Oh, well, yes of course…" She paused, then added, "And Mr Harward's ball? When is it to be?"

Roberta frowned and replied, "It is to be Wednesday fortnight…. though I do wonder if the rooms are large enough to hold a ball. I have seen very little inside, of course, but Partridge Lodge is not so very grand as to accommodate thirty dancing guests."

"You know as well as I do," replied Mariah doubtingly, "it is a rare ball indeed if all the guests are dancing… I do believe… I have never attended such a ball in all my life."

Roberta nodded in agreement. "That is true… but have you not received a card?" Mariah shook her head. For several moments, Roberta was silent and watched her friend.

"My dear one, you must tell me… is anything the matter?" Mariah shook her head. "Did something happen in London? Are you being reserved with me? I cannot tell these days; I know I am forgetful of late… are you well?" Mariah assured her she was most well, but that Aunt Mary was not. Roberta asked if it was anything serious and if the doctor had been called and at length assumed that this must be the cause of Mariah's low spirits. Mariah assured her that it was nothing very serious.

Though Mariah and Aunt Mary had been restricted to the ground floor since their return home, there was an old pianoforte in the parlour that Mariah had not used in some time, but Edward had kept it in good condition. That afternoon, she sat down at the instrument and began to play. After a little while, checking on her aunt occasionally, as she still was not feeling much better, there was a knock on the door. She stopped playing and got up to answer it, but a maid swiftly responded before she had even reached the vestibule. It was a servant delivering a letter. The notepaper colour and writing were familiar to Mariah and she stopped the maid before it could be taken upstairs. "One moment, please... I believe that is for me, from Lady Coburn. Indeed, I recognise the hand."

"Begging your pardon, miss, but all mail is to be taken to the Mistress first," replied the maid.

"Unless... it is addressed to myself! Would you please check the address," replied Mariah, a little annoyed at being immediately denied her own letter. Upon checking, it was clear the letter was addressed to Mariah and the maid reluctantly gave it over. Mariah began to think more bitterly of Elizabeth's demands and wondered what business her own letters were to anyone else, especially as Elizabeth's actions could be viewed as little more than a contemptible intrusion of privacy.

Mariah paused long in the parlour without opening the letter and she took deep breaths to calm her growing angst. She was sure she knew what the letter would contain; that it was of an unpleasant nature she had little doubt, and thought herself fortunate on one point at least that she had been there to intercept her own letter.

Though Lady Coburn had been a near acquaintance for many years, Mariah had always been treated with special courtesy and of high regard. In spite of a near acquaintance though, the uncle had been severe and she thought it probable the letter contained an admonishment at the very least, or at the worst, possible exclusion from the Grey's Musical Society, by consequence of her actions and the uncle's condemnation. Mariah bit her lip, and walked to her room with the unopened letter, bracingly grateful to find Aunt Mary was sleeping still.

Painstakingly, so as not to wake her aunt, Mariah very gently tore the seal and unfolded the letter; a small card fell out to the floor. She picked it up and stared at in disbelief; it was an invitation to a Musical Evening at Chifley Grey House. She looked at it again in astonishment; surely there was some mistake. She read the letter more eagerly, hesitating at every new paragraph for the expected reproach, but it contained nothing of the kind. Moreover, the letter, as well as kindly, expressly invited Mariah and her aunt to dine with them before the Musical Evening.

Mariah shook her head in disbelief; that Lady Coburn did not know of what had occurred in London seemed impossible; surely Sir Niels had written of his reproofs of Mariah's character and conduct. She dreaded to think that any day now Lady Coburn would receive word from London and wish to recant the invitation. Moreover, that a second letter would be received to rescind the first and if she was not by, Elizabeth could intercept it. Mariah immediately pondered how it might be avoided but here she considered with relief that Edward's return would end or at least relieve their present constraint. It was possible to put off an answer for several days, at least until after her brother's return.

On the Monday, Elizabeth made a show of welcoming her husband home in front of her noble guests, but no one was more glad to see him, than his sister and aunt.

As soon as he was able to escape from the company of his wife and her guests, he went downstairs to see Mariah and

Aunt Mary. Though they did not wish to burden him after a long journey, he assured them both that he was more than up to the task of hearing them out, as he had already had two letters from Uncle John.

When they had finished telling him all very modestly, as they did not wish to make things terrible betwixt husband and wife, Edward was silent and grave. Aunt Mary thought that perhaps they had not said enough, while Mariah believed they had been too harsh and said too much. But it was no surprise to anyone that while the "Noble guests of Ramsgate" went for a walk to the Forbury Gardens that afternoon, a loud row could be heard from an upstairs room.

After a grand feast the night before enjoyed by all, on account of it being a final evening for Elizabeth's guests and the return of her husband, the guests departed early the following day. Edward's severe reproofs of his wife's keeping house were swiftly attended to and Mariah and Aunt Mary were restored to their second-floor bedrooms that afternoon. Aunt Mary had only one complaint, for she could not fault Elizabeth on the new carpets, only that the new wallpaper was too plain.

Chapter Eight

Mariah had made up her mind not to attend the Musical Evening at Chifley Grey House, or the dinner or indeed share any part of the invitation with her aunt. Now that Edward had returned and Aunt Mary was once more feeling better, it was safe to send letters without the fear of breach of privacy, but Mariah had still not replied. Her vexation and anxiety grew with each passing day; she expected a recant of invitation and a scolding from Lady Coburn, but no scolding came.

***

The Thursday before the Musical Evening at Chifley Grey House, Mariah having still not replied, Lady Coburn happened upon her at the Rectory.

"Oh, Miss Mariah, I was beginning to think that reports of your return were quite mistaken, save Mrs Marsh telling me that she had indeed met with you. I was quite envious that she had taken tea with you and I had not. And why have you not answered my letter?" said Lady Coburn happily.

Mariah blushed and smiled and wondered what she ought to say.

"Well, never mind, I expect you have had much to do. Of course, I will take seeing you today as confirmation of your attendance. You will be most pleased, half the town has been invited, of course, but I must have my leading pianist to show off." Lady Coburn was all smiles. Mariah only laughed timidly. "I have been most anxious to have professionals from London, no less, four of the hirelings are musicians and three glee singers." Mariah nodded her enthusiasm; it did sound to her as if it would certainly be a splendid evening. "I knew you would be pleased. I am so glad you will come, but you must excuse me just now, as I have business with the chaplain." Lady Coburn then strode off in the direction of the church, leaving Mariah to return home.

***

Mrs Marsh, having received a note from Partridge Lodge, was eager to speak with Mariah as soon as may be.

"Oh, my dear one, we have been invited to an afternoon at Partridge Lodge tomorrow."

"How lovely for you both," replied Mariah relieved that she was to be spared any duty, but Roberta laughed.

"Oh, no… I meant you and me, silly. Miss Harward has come to keep house for her brother and desires to make our acquaintance."

"Oh! I see, how charming." Mariah nodded awkwardly, trying not to show her immediate disappointment. "But has not Mr Marsh gone to Town? And how are you feeling? Are you well enough to walk a three-quarter mile?"

Roberta assured her that Mr M would very much wish her to be in company and more too, she had not felt any sickness now for many weeks, though she could not stop eating the delightfully sweet strawberries the Miss Fannings brought her t'other day with salty ham, and then in a mild rebuke chastised her friend for cleverly changing the topic. She only added that as the gentlemen would not be about that afternoon, if they remained long, and she was certain it need not be too long, the gentlemen would return from their shooting by and by.

"Roberta!" replied Mariah with slight disapproval.

"Well…. Miss Harward was with her brother when they called on us Monday. Such a pretty thing too, and so polite, but you will see for yourself tomorrow. I am sure you will soon love her as a sister." Mariah tried very hard not to sigh too loudly and with reluctance dutifully submitted to the scheme.

At Mrs Marsh's insistence, they arrived at Partridge Lodge the following day by carriage. Mariah was pleased that Roberta had agreed to its use; as she was, by her own admission, in her sixth month. Mariah observed that Mrs Marsh's description of Mr Harward's sister had been accurate. Miss Alexina Harward, the youngest sibling of Mr Harward, was tall and blonde like her brother, and though not slight, she was refined, courteous, happily affable and judging by her table, accustomed to playing hostess.

It was pleasant company, but both Mrs Marsh and Mariah were surprised to find that Miss Harward could neither play nor sing. Mariah recalled Mr Harward saying on the first meeting that there was no music in his house. Miss Harward was so overjoyed that they could both play and sing and she asked them to sing her something directly. The ladies declined as there was no instrument for the key, but Miss Harward was steadily persistent. Unable to refuse Miss Harward's continued urgings, they sang her a very short Irish Air. Miss Harward thought it was the most wonderful thing she had ever heard.

Miss Harward's eagerness for women's companionship meant she was not in haste for her new friends to take leave, and several rounds of refreshments followed the first. Moreover, by Mrs Marsh's secret desire, they dallied longer still at Partridge Lodge. The latter all the while ignoring Mariah's hints to be gone. Like the refreshments, the conversation did not dwindle either, because if Mrs Marsh was not speaking, Miss Harward certainly was, and though neither required any input from Mariah, Mrs Marsh frequently forced Mariah to speak through an account or acknowledgement of accomplishment or attendance till Mariah was heartily sick of speaking of herself.

Mariah could not determine if she was more thankful for the appearance of the returned gentlemen late that afternoon, as her detainment was over and a welcome relief in the change of company, or dreading the steady resistance to his advances and vexation at their combined scheming.

Now was their chance to take leave and in standing up and moving towards her friend, she was greeted warmly by Mr Harward himself; but she had no time for speeches or to catch Roberta's eye, because at that very moment, Mr Harward, with vigorous enthusiasm, entreated them both to stay.

"Ladies… You must dine with us this evening, I mean to treat you all, we have such a fine delicacy of teal and partridge for pie. I remark so because several of which are by my own hand, though the deed itself is the dominion of men, it should impress a lady that he has triumphed in his quest by stock and aim," said he, his fellow hunting party in agreeance; the invitation was seconded by his sister and Roberta happily and readily accepted for them both.

Unlikely as it was, Mariah's evening was not altogether unpleasant. Mr Harward's uncle was refreshingly different in his approach to civilities; he had not his intentions secreted in every look, speech and action. She was relieved to find him pleasant and had high hopes they would yet make charming neighbours and even relations if it came to that; till he made a third and fourth mention of his brother's estate in Brighton; its grandness, the expanse of windows, three very large dining halls, a long avenue of maples, and a view from the third story windows all the way to the sea. Mr Harward, however, saw it all with pleasure and took it as a good omen of her particular interest in his family.

In quiet reflection over the next few days, Mariah prayerfully contemplated the consequence of Mr Harward's growing attentions to herself. Unmarried, she was reminded by her brother's wife, daily, of the delicateness of her situation, eroding her very respectability and advantage. Marriage, however, would secure her place in society, the wife of a respectable gentleman, or so she was continually reminded, and with scarcely any change to her comforts. Moreover, aside from his high praises to herself and his diligence and approval of everybody, she could not find reasons for her displeasure of his intimate company.

Mariah also began to consider that perhaps her own estimations of his character were misled by his fervent perseverance. Though she could never feel the same way as she did for Frederick Tenby, his charm and character were far superior to any other man she had ever met. But at length, she reproached herself for her happy delusion, she must not think of him, and she recalled with acute pains that the union would never be sanctioned by any of his relations. He was very soon to be the spouse of another, and perhaps in time, she would esteem Mr Harward.

***

The following Tuesday, at Lady Coburn's dinner, Mariah was surprised and pleased to find that she and her aunt were not the only particular guests for the dinner. The Normans and the Reverend Green and his wife had also been favoured with a dinner before the musical performance.

Mrs Green spoke of her disappointment that her beautiful old harp had been damaged by the youths and she was sure it would cost more than twenty pounds to repair, and for the foreseeable future she would not be able to play with the Grey's Musical Society. This was immediately disputed by the others and Lady Coburn herself offered her own spare harp for the cause until Mrs Green's was suitably repaired. The Reverend thought this too much, his wife was all gratitude and Lady Coburn steadily insisted. While Mrs Norman could not wait to tell them all of their plans to go to Bath for the winter, on account of Mr Norman's brother having taken a house in Beaufort Square. Sir Arthur and Lady Coburn, however, were all friendliness and ease, pleased to be hosting a grand affair.

When the second dishes where cleared away, Mrs Norman had opportunity to speak with Mariah alone and could not help but give Mariah a little hint of what she had heard of her ventures in London. That Mariah had been seen with Lady Coburn's own brother. Mariah turned pale and looked to Lady Coburn to see if they had been overheard, but they had not. On enquiring how Mrs Norman came by this news, she discovered, to her immense relief, that it was a second-hand account, and with delicacy expressed to Mrs Norman that she was wholly mistaken and that there must be some confusion with his betrothed, Miss Harper. Mrs Norman was momentarily silent but was then astonished, for Lady Coburn had not mentioned that her dearest brother was to be married. It was then small comfort to Mariah to know that Mrs Norman had not spoken with Lady Coburn on the matter. Mariah hastily added her hopes that Mrs Norman would not voice her mistaken surprise to Lady Coburn, to which Mrs Norman reluctantly agreed she would not.

The next morning, the day of Mr Harward's ball, there was a great commotion. Mrs Dunmead's dress had arrived, but she was dissatisfied with her ordered gown, she was vexed by its plainness and felt it unbecoming of a lady in her situation. Mariah heard all this without leaving her room, but the next moment the disturbance was brought to her immediate notice, as Mrs Dunmead burst into her room.

"Oh Mariah," wailed Mrs Dunmead. "You must tell me your opinion; it is too plain, is it not?"

"It is an elegant dress, and it is your colour, though a little plain, but surely a little lace on the sleeves would suffice?" Mariah smiled.

"That is just what I thought. Only it is too late to be sent out," replied Mrs Dunmead, "You must do it for me, my eyes are too weak, you see, and I must attend to more important matters just now..." She paused, though Mariah was too surprised to reply. Mrs Dunmead only added, "You are so kind, I don't know what I'd do otherwise." She then handed

Mariah gown and lace and quit the room, closing the door behind her.

Mariah spent all morning delicately stitching the lace to the gown as best she could; though she could stitch well enough, she had not the expertise and flair of Mrs Marsh and at several points bled her fingers. When it was done, she placed it in Mrs Dunmead's room only to discover that another two new gowns were also displayed, with trimmings on! Mariah could not understand it, and though she thought it very odd, now was not the time to consider it at any length. She had neglected her own toilette and preparations for the ball and now had no time to gather shoe roses or flowers.

At the ball that evening, the duties expected by her were not unforeseen by Mariah, and she knew that it would give much pleasure to her friends and family to see her honoured at Mr Harward's ball. She was grateful that neither the room nor the guest list was very large. Mr Harward was, in turn, all expectation at the promise of the first dance with Mariah.

Her immediate duty performed, she smiled courteously and went away in hopes of finding and sharing in Mrs Marsh's hidden corner of the room. At length, she found Roberta in the little east parlour eating cake.

"I saw you all dancing just now. Oh, you look nice…" She then stopped suddenly and added, "but my dear one, it is not like you to overlook shoe roses, and you have no adornments for your hair." Roberta then abused her friend for their absence, for she was not yet married, and it would not do to not look one's best. Mariah sighed and explained her day's work. Roberta, though astonished, could no more give explanations than Mariah.

Roberta was then quick to add that though she would allow her friend to stay by as Mariah could not dance every dance, she ought not hide away in the parlour reserved for the old married women. Mariah nodded and agreed she would not.

After several dances, Mariah returned to her friend.

"Oh, my dear one, you must assist me, please, and open that window. My estimation to you the other day was accurate, you know. I do believe Mr Harward has overestimated the size of the rooms, they are far too small for dancing in, after all. I was very nearly all but overcome from the heat. I am sure if I had not you by me, I should have succumbed." Mariah sympathised with her friend and opened the windows as she was bid. "When you are Mistress of this house, I will rely on you, my dear one, you must talk him out of such foolishness." Mariah only smiled.

Sometime later, Mariah watched Mrs Dunmead dance and smiled; despite Mr Harward's previous slight of her dancing, she really was quite graceful going down the dance. Mariah then observed her Aunt and Uncle Matlock, who were dancing together, and her eyes then perused the room with particular notice as to its size and was just deciding that Mrs Marsh's previous impression had been just when she saw with some surprise the dour face of another observer. Elizabeth's eyes followed her mother with bitter loathing. Mariah was taken aback and looked about to see if others observed Elizabeth's apparent disapproval. More too she feared that there may be another row on the morrow as Mrs Dunmead had danced many of the dances, and Elizabeth's looks were unmistakably severe.

Early the next morning Mariah rose to take in a walk as she had arranged with Mrs Marsh, in hopes of avoiding the expected row. She accompanied one of the maids to the corner and then walked in the direction of Minster Street to call on Mrs Marsh and together they planned to spend at least an hour along the river and in the gardens and hoped that this would not be too much for her friend.

After remaining an additional half hour with Mrs Marsh at her Minster Street Terrace, Mariah returned home via West Street and was surprised to see Mr Harward riding in the direction of the Oxford road. His coat and figure were unmistakable, but his distance and speed were too great for polite greeting and she continued on toward her own home in anticipation of a cold welcome. Nothing could have been further from the truth. Everyone, especially Mrs Dunmead, was in good spirits and amicable, and she happily joined them.

Chapter Nine

A particularly cool October presented many social engagements for the residents of Reading, public balls were often announced with the occasional evening assembly some days following. For Mariah, however, and those dearly and even not so dearly acquainted with Mr Harward, not a week passed without some invitation or card requesting the company of herself and her family to Partridge Lodge and its gardens while the sun lasted.

The parties themselves were pleasant enough, though Mr Harward's attentions were steadfast to herself, the new company was tolerable, the familiar company pleasing and Mariah bore it much better with Mrs Marsh.

By mid-October, however, Mrs Marsh's attendance was beginning to wane. It was not unexpected as Mrs Marsh was nearing her confinement, but Mariah would miss the refuge of her company all the same.

Mariah and the Miss Fannings were then often obliged to sit with Miss Harward and listen to her tell the same stories and the same news she spoke of the last time they were together, with scarcely a breath from one sentence to the next. Her only other choice besides being in a conversation with Edward and Elizabeth, which usually ended with the latter keenly asserting her superiority, was to join her Aunt Anna, Mrs Matlock and the cheerful Mrs Fanning on the settee in the corner. Unless, of course, the object was cards, in which she was almost always required to partner Mr Harward or his sister herself at their insistence.

One morning after a particularly successful evening at cards for Mariah, Edward approached his sister in the parlour, while she was alone after breakfast.

"I know you were sincere in your speech to me in June when we last spoke of the matter, and I think it natural that you have changed your mind, as I have been led to believe. But you need not hold back on my account. My dear sister, I will not think less of you because of it. Indeed, you must make allowances for admiration now that it has come. It is not unusual when two people have been thrown together as often as you two have of late."

"You are speaking of Mr Harward?" asked Mariah.

"Indeed, I am! Though I am sorry if it gives you pain." Mariah's sudden look of weariness on the subject did not escape him, he could not be unfeeling but he very much desired to give her counsel, and to give her leave to submit to his admiration, which he understood, she did return. "But you have always been cautious in love, and I'm afraid by my example, more cautious still. But it need not be so. I will gladly approve of the match if it is what you wish."

"Cautious?" Mariah replied tentatively. "Oh, no… it is not cautiousness that prevents me… it is a deficiency of admiration."

"Deficiency?" Edward almost laughed. "Let me assure you, my dear sister," replied her brother firmly and with feeling, "perhaps you do not know your own heart, anyone that has seen you two together would have no doubt of its being so… But come, I will not send you, my dear Mariah, with haste into marriage, though you are twenty-seven. I would, however, recommend some serious time of reflection to assist you to make the right decision sooner. I do not know how long Mr Harward is likely to wait. There is talk of him going away after Christmas, and there is no knowing when he will return, but I do have doubts of him, at that time… being unwed still, you understand me?" He looked at her face with kindness trying to catch her eye, but she would not look up.

Mariah tried very hard not to sigh and nodded her acknowledgement of her brother's wishes and Edward, trusting to Mariah's sensible nature, believed he had performed his duty, so as to bring about the match sooner.

Mariah did as her brother wished and by degrees allowed herself to be more willingly accepting of Mr Harward's compliments and more agreeable to his wishes; if nothing else Mr Harward had all the appearance of sincerity. Though she really began to feel her society at home and at Partridge Lodge confined and unchanging, she submitted to its tediousness by degrees and even allowed herself to be guided by Mr Harward on one or two subjects of no real importance.

Aunt Mary joined Mariah for the morning service on Sunday, where they were both invited to call on Lady Coburn thereafter.

"You both have been dearly missed," said Lady Coburn, "it has been a fortnight at the very least."

"And it feels longer still, I assure you," replied Aunt Mary. Sir Arthur smirked from behind his paper.

"Oh yes, you must forgive our absence, your ladyship, my time… our time has not been our own for some weeks."

"Oh, well, duties must be done, I suppose. But I would much prefer your company to myself," smiled Lady Coburn.

"Mutual as our feelings are, your ladyship," said Aunt Mary "regrettably, Mariah has been a pawn to the schemes of another."

"Aunt…" said Mariah, in a tone of slight disapproval.

"Truly? Does the gentleman not know he is being schemed upon?" Mariah blushed. "You need not speak his name," added Lady Coburn, unaware that Mariah was being courted.

"Oh no, I'm afraid the scheme is not at all welcome," added Aunt Mary.

"Oh," replied Lady Coburn, who now understood the distress. "Well, then you'll be pleased to have a new excuse because it is essential that you are here. We must begin our pieces for the Christmas soirée. And as we shan't have Mrs Marsh, and Mrs Green is all thumbs on the spare harp, I will be relying on you to lead the melody." Mariah smiled, and Aunt Mary looked quite pleased for any excuse to spend time in the company of others.

"You are very kind," said Mariah.

"Kindness! No indeed. It is much more than kindness, for you are very much wanted." Lady Coburn grinned sheepishly. "And of course, and we all of us, take great delight in your talent. And therefore, must take every advantage while you are still single, my dear." Mariah blushed and smiled politely.

Before Mariah and Aunt Mary left Chifley Grey House, Lady Coburn reminded her guest that she would see them on Tuesday.

"Sir Arthur will send for you at three o'clock on Tuesday as usual," said she.

"This Tuesday? So soon?" asked Mariah

"Yes, my dear, we must make haste." Mariah looked a little surprised. "There is to be a special party at Christmas on account of some particular guests from London."

"Oh, I see." Mariah smiled impassively.

"Oh, did I not say? My brother and our cousins the Proberts are coming to stay with us, I believe you met them when you were last in London." Mariah nodded, said that she had and bid the good lady farewell.

Mariah and Aunt Mary rode home in silence. Mariah considered how strange that Mr Tenby did not bring his betrothed, at least she would not have that pain. Perhaps Lady Coburn did not think to mention it because they were already married and by assumption, his wife would be with him. Mariah sighed; it made her ill to think on it any longer.

The following week brought Mariah fresh agonies; a dinner party at Addison Terrace to which the usual guests were all invited. Mr Harward was very pointedly sat by Mariah at table, the furthest end from Edward, while Elizabeth and the Matlocks sat by Edward. After dinner when the gentlemen rejoined the ladies in the parlour, the Miss Fannings were invited to play. Mr Matlock, keen to discuss a favoured interest with Colonel Fanning, dared to play opposite him at cards.

"I'm not one especially for chasing excitement, Colonel Fanning, but what's this I hear about a superior horse at a race meet next week?" said Mr Matlock. The Colonel laughed.

"Indeed, I have been contemplating the notion of making the journey to Bostworth Common next week," confessed the Colonel.

"Is that so? Then what you say is of interest to me, for you've always had an eye for picking a good horse, you know," replied Mr Matlock.

"Bostworth Common?" queried Mr Harward. "Is not that near Burghfield? My uncle has an acquaintance not far from there."

"It is indeed sir…" replied the Colonel.

"There is also a track for lesser-known horses, Mr Harward," added Mrs Matlock, "Do you like the sport in general? Are you a devotee?"

"Oh, utterly," replied Mr Harward. Mrs Matlock looked to her husband smilingly.

"I think, I should very much like to go, John," said his wife quietly.

"And you'd be very welcome. The more the merrier, Mrs Matlock," added the Colonel.

"Oh, Edward, why do we not all go?" added Elizabeth. "I am quite partial to the thrill of a little horse racing now and then."

"I see," said Edward to his wife, "should we all go, Colonel?"

"We could make a proper time of it," replied the Colonel.

"Is it very far?" asked Mr Harward.

"Not at all, not at all," replied the Colonel.

"It's about eight miles from here," said Edward.

"Nine and one half if you go through Burghfield," said Mr Matlock. "But somehow, we never do."

It was soon decided by the Colonel's information that they would travel down on the Monday for the meet, and stay until Thursday, as the Ardleforth Cup was on the Wednesday.

Mariah was disheartened; she felt sorely the disappointment of missing a Tuesday's rehearsal and the additional work it meant for her own practice and the anticipation of Lady Coburn's displeasure. She attempted, without much success at being heard, to give good reasons to remain at home with Aunt Mary, but they were all of them ignored by both her brother and his wife. So, to Bostworth she would go.

Chapter Ten

The journey thither was easy and uneventful and they arrived in time to lay odds and spectate the race, but their view was partly hindered by the crowds of people they found there. Edward shared his astonishment with Mariah to see so many people. After some thought, Edward's only suggestion was that they had misjudged the significance of the race and the renown of the Ardleforth Cup. This view was accepted and shared by Colonel Fanning and Mr Matlock; they too could only arrive at the same conclusion.

They were inconvenienced further still as their preferred lodgings, which had always been the White Crown in that part of the country, had no rooms available. They then made enquiries at the Saddler's Arms, a short distance down the High Street, where there were several moderately comfortable rooms available, but only two first-class rooms remained. Elizabeth determined on one of the best rooms available directly and made it very plain, to all her company, that she had no intention of sharing her good fortune. Mariah was encouraged to lodge with her Aunt and Uncle Matlock, and Mrs Dunmead took a moderately comfortable room for herself.

It wasn't until their second day in Bostworth that they learned of the reason for the crowds. The reported arrival of a well-known composer from Bavaria for a private concert had brought throngs of crowds to the area, which in turn took advantage of the local races by day and the best of the inns by night.

The Colonel, through an acquaintance, secured box seating at the race meet for the ladies and from their seats, they saw it all; the preparation of the participants, the swell of the spectating crowds, and the occasional eruption of enthusiasm.

After the third race of the day, Mrs Matlock thought she saw a familiar figure in raptures below. "Is that... Mr Harward?" said she, surprised. Straining her eyes Elizabeth attempted to make him out. Mariah looked in the direction Mrs Matlock had indicated below. "By the man there, with the green top hat," added she. Mariah nodded and agreed that it did indeed bear a marked resemblance to Mr Harward.

"Oh yes, I see, It does look like him. But I cannot be sure," said Mariah; she could not make out his form and dress enough to convince her of its truth.

"Surely! It is him," declared Mrs Dunmead with certainty, "He wears that blue and silver coat everywhere." Then added a little more quietly to herself, "It is a particular shade of blue..."

"Well, if it is Mr Harward, he appears to be very pleased with himself," said Elizabeth. "You should go to him, Mariah, he appears to be a little impetuous, who knows what he might do in such elation?" Mariah winced. Mrs Dunmead looked embarrassed by her daughter, while Mrs Fanning and Mrs Matlock admonished Elizabeth with their joined looks. Mrs Matlock's shock was so disapproving she instantly gave her opinion, very decidedly, against forming any such plan of an impulsive and imprudent nature. Mrs Fanning too thought it a rash and foolish thing to do. The older ladies were relieved that Mariah made no change from her seat, for she was more inclined to the advice of a beloved aunt than the provocation of a sister relation. Mariah smiled at her aunt and made no answer.

"Oh, for shame," cried Elizabeth, "it was only a little joke. You are too severe upon me, 'tis of no consequence; I knew, of course, Mariah would not..." Elizabeth smiled at them all in turn, "she never does as she's told, you know... so you see, of course, I knew she would not take me at my word."

It amazed Mrs Matlock and Mrs Fanning to hear Elizabeth speak so and wondered if she had taken leave of her senses. Mrs Matlock looked to Mrs Dunmead to rebuke her daughter's stupidity, but Mrs Dunmead was still watching the figure they had now confirmed to be Mr Harward.

Mrs Matlock paused and looked to Mariah and quietly added, "If your Aunt Mary were here, I believe she would advise against both action and speeches made in haste, theirs is a propensity for regret." Mariah smiled and acknowledged the truth of it.

It astonished Mrs Matlock and Mrs Fanning further still, when not a quarter hour later, Mrs Dunmead quit the stand entirely, stating that she had business with the little haberdasher in the Bostworth High Street. Elizabeth, seeing their confused faces, explained it away, stating that her mother was always on the lookout for new dresses.

Later that afternoon when they were all dining together at the inn, the Colonel was in low spirits and quite put out by the shamefully exorbitant stake Mr Harward had placed against the horse that not only beat his favourite but had won. There were several murmurs around the table. Mr Matlock, however, misunderstood the Colonel's attack on Mr Harward's win as merely sour grapes and asserted that while winning is the best of times, defeat can make us unjustly severe. For surely the sum was not so great as to censure a character. The Colonel assured him it was, Edward nodded gravely and Mr Matlock enquired how much. There were general gasps of astonishment when the Colonel confessed that he did not know exactly, but that it was in excess of two thousand pounds.

"Surely not!" exclaimed Mr Matlock. "My good fellow, that is a gravely shocking thing to say, can you be sure that it is truth…? Surely, we ought not to speak ill of the man who devised the whole of our journey… besides, it is unconscionable, he is not here, and therefore cannot defend or refute himself against these accusations."

Mrs Matlock and Mrs Fanning agreed. Mariah had not noticed his absence till that moment and looked around the table, but Mr Harward was not there, and she was immediately gratified by the discovery. Evidently, this was also news to Elizabeth as she too appeared to be astonished by his absence.

The following day, when Elizabeth had gone out with Mrs Fanning and Mrs Matlock for a walk among the flowers in the common, Edward summoned his sister to his room.

"What is it, Edward? Are you ill, you do look pale, are you well?" queried Mariah as soon as she had come.

"Calm yourself, my dear sister, it is just the pork pies, I've eaten too many, you see, they are too good, and I rarely indulge." Mariah smirked, and he sat down in a comfortable chair.

"Then what is it?" asked she.

"Will you be very angry with me if I withdraw my permission… That is to say, I have changed my mind. Tell me… it is not too late, I am not too late." Edward sighed long and asked for a glass of ale to be brought up.

"What is too late? You are not making any sense," and she propped him up with some pillows to make him comfortable. "There, will that do?" Edward nodded. "Now…speak plainly, Edward." Mariah was perplexed by his meaning and his insinuation.

"Very well," said he, pulling at his necktie, "as wretched as the account is, it has done Mr Harward no favours on recommendations; quite the reverse. Mariah, let us not deceive ourselves, your ears are as good as mine, so you heard it all last night, and you know what that means?" Mariah nodded. "I have judged his weaknesses ill. His ceaseless flattery has concealed his deficiencies from us all." Edward paused and in a softer voice added, "But despite all this, worse still, would be the dreaded news… Oh, it gives me pain to even confess it, that I wished for it…. I am now to learn that he is to be my brother…"

"Oh no, Edward, there is no engagement, no understanding betwixt us at all, you need not worry yourself, I am not bound by any promise of the kind. I have been spared the decision entirely." Her brother looked perplexed. "He has not asked me, Edward." Edward looked relieved.

"Oh, Mariah, can you ever forgive my strong cautions to you?"

"There is nothing to forgive… How are you to blame for his unending flattery and senseless actions? He has done it entirely by his own will."

"Perhaps not, but I regret my previous encouragement to you all the same. And I pray, thank God, that you, dear sister, are more steadfast then I. You have not been deluded by flattery, and charmed by deceit. You truly are to be admired for your courage. But a gamester will never be admitted into the family. I promised our father that I would see you right. And I shall!"

"Of course you shall, I have never doubted it, Edward… but here is your ale, you had better drink it! And you must rest… and no more pork pies." Edward agreed that he had indulged enough.

Later that morning, Mr Harward, in high spirits, boldly pressed all his companions to remain at Bostworth for one more day, lest they regret a very favoured opportunity. For he had expressly received an invitation for them all to a private concert that very evening. The Colonel, whether by animosity on account of Mr Harward's win and his own loss, or an impatience to be home again, politely declined the offer and insisted they would leave as planned. Edward too was inclined to leave, but his wife's eagerness to be in high society, especially when, as Mr Harward had said they were particularly invited, was not worth the injunction.

The concert was in a moderately sized hall of a great house in that part of the country. Though the rest of the party did not know their destination, the little convoy of two carriages and a spare easily followed Mr Harward's uncle's carriage to the Great Hall, not a three-quarter mile from the common.

"I do wonder at our invitation," whispered Mariah's Aunt Anna to her as they were ushered inside.

"How so?" replied Mariah in equally hushed tones.

"Well for one, in my experience at least… composers, famous or not, are not generally open to usurpers such as ourselves." Mariah had not considered this 'til now and her hesitation at what the evening might bring increased.

"You feel it too?" added Mariah. Her Aunt Anna nodded.

"And I have not seen halls decorated in this style since my youth…" she paused for a more minute inspection… "though well maintained, it is less than what someone of high society might expect…" Mariah nodded her agreement and remained close to her Aunt Anna till they were seated along with at least thirty other guests. Mr Harward assumed the seat by Mariah and shortly thereafter, five musicians took their places. In the corner where the shadows were greater sat the pianist, but try as they might, neither Mariah nor her aunt could make him out.

After the first piece was played, Mr Harward excused himself, presumably, thought Mariah, to speak with the host.

"Did you recognise that piece?" whispered Mrs Matlock to Mariah, who shook her head. "Pleasant as it was, it was well played, though nothing compared to the greats… of course, It is not a piece that either your Uncle John or myself recognise, what are your thoughts?"

"I caught a glimpse of his grey hair, at the end of the piece, but I cannot make him out."

"No, nor I. I think it must be a little ruse," smirked Mrs Matlock to her niece, "a blind ploy if you will, based on the rumours that were all alive on Tuesday. What think you?" Mariah nodded.

Both Mariah and her aunt and uncle began to suspect the musician was ill qualified to play, let alone compose his own pieces.

"This is hardly the work of any famous musician I know… I certainly hope our Mr Harward has not paid out excessively for these tickets…" added her uncle after the third piece. Mariah confessed she knew nothing about it.

There was much murmuring among the guests when several familiar pieces were played which culminated in the recompense and speedy departure of some of the guests during the short interval.

Some singing then followed before more unfamiliar pieces were played.

At the end of the evening, while they waited for their carriages, Mrs Dunmead expressed her delight at the evening's entertainment, and she would be very grateful if anyone could tell her whom she had had the pleasure of listening to as she was none the wiser. Mrs Matlock looked to Mariah to hide her smile.

"I hardly know why, Mother, you were not present for more than half of the concert," mocked Elizabeth.

"I could hear it very well from the back, thank you, it was the wine—it made me feel quite ill, and I needed some air."

"Oh, quite so," added Mr Harward, smiling broadly. "Ghastly brew!" Mariah and Mrs Matlock turned in surprise at his voice and his return. They, neither of them, had noticed his reappearance.

Chapter Eleven

Late the following morning, they were all preparing to leave when Edward was in receipt of an urgent letter. After several moments, he advised them all that they were to go on without him, as he had some business that would delay him an hour or so in Burghfield.

Mariah assumed that without Edward, Elizabeth's preference would be for her and her mother to travel alone and she immediately approached her Aunt Anna and Uncle John. Elizabeth acknowledged her thoughtfulness, and her aunt and uncle, of course, welcomed her additional company gladly.

They began their journey, and on reaching the main road, Mr Matlock promptly made himself comfortable in a corner of the carriage and was soon softly snoring.

"I cannot understand it!" began Mariah's Aunt Anna in a low voice, once her husband had fallen asleep.

"What confuses you, Aunt?" asked Mariah, thinking she wished to again discuss the previous evening.

"Why you, my dear…! Pardon my interference, but I must confess my surprise at you being unattached, still…"

"Oh well, I suppose it is just that way with some women; take Aunt Mary, for example, she is perfectly content in her spinsterhood…"

"Indeed she is!" smiled her Aunt Anna. "But I am talking of opportunities lost. And I must give credit where it is due, even if you are my niece and my proclivities are all for your success."

"Oh…" replied Mariah quietly, and looked out the window.

"I beg you will hear me out…" pleaded her Aunt Anna kindly. Mariah returned her gaze to her aunt and smiled respectfully. "You must see it as your uncle and I do, for we are both most anxious for your happiness…" She paused again. "And you, well, you are neither plain nor so poor, with ten thousand pounds on your marriage and though I myself cannot claim to have equal frankness with you, or that I am aware of all your preferences by and by, you appear to us determined to evade it all… Is there some impediment or objection to an attachment, or even to the gentleman?" Mariah made no answer. Her aunt then added in a kinder and softer voice, "Then let me encourage you, as one who has nothing but familiar interest in your success and nothing to gain… Do not wait for perfection any longer, but take hold of this opportunity that is given you, happiness… can be found without it, I assure you."

"Oh Aunt, I do see what you mean. And if it were only that which prevented me, I would agree to marry tomorrow… but I desire so much more." Mariah sighed and was on the verge of declaring her renewed mark of dislike on account of his recent high and imprudent outlay, which her aunt and uncle had disbelieved and thought it all talk from the start when what followed, her aunt's reply, delayed any further discourse on the subject.

"Oh of course… I know, my dear, all young ladies desire it so, but you are not so young, and there is danger in waiting too long." Mariah paused, for just at that moment her Uncle John stirred; they had reached the Castle Road.

Later that day, after the evening meal, Elizabeth took up the new fashion pamphlet in the upstairs parlour awaiting her husband's arrival, while Mariah filled in her Aunt Mary on all their Bostworth adventures.

Then suddenly, their evening was interrupted by an urgent message received at the door. It was for Elizabeth. There had been an accident and Edward had been thrown from his horse by the Olde Bridge. Elizabeth immediately cried out, Mrs Dunmead came running, and the whole house was seized with alarm. Elizabeth fainted and was carried to her room, closely followed by her mother, who attended her. Mariah too felt the foreboding dread of this news but thanked the doctor's son, Master Poole, as he agreed to wait while she fetched her bonnet and shawl.

"Oh Mariah!" said Aunt Mary stiffly. "Quickly, my dear, you must bring him here if you can. I dare say the people who attend him are full of good intentions, but I know he would much prefer to be here." Mariah hesitated, too shocked to reply and Aunt Mary added, "Quickly now, Elizabeth surely cannot!" scoffed Aunt Mary. "Taken with hysterics! Let her rest!" She paused again, but Mariah was out the door and following Master Poole to the Olde Bridge.

Mariah hurried along behind him, her alarm increasing with every step. The scene was a horrible wreck! Mariah trembled with fear to see a badly wounded Edward lying motionless on boards. Dr Poole was anxious that Mariah should not witness the scene and attempted to shield her view.

Mariah, however ill she might feel at the sight, was determined to be of assistance and assured him she was quite prepared for it. But Dr Poole would not be talked out of his dislike of her presence and impressed upon her the importance that she would be of better use making preparations at home. Edward's arm and leg were in need of manipulation and his head, several bandages. On the doctor's authority, the latter given to Mariah herself, Edward was to be brought to Addison Terrace, in need of a quiet room, where he could be kept still, with warm fire against the chill.

By the following morning, Elizabeth could not stir herself past her own room and Mrs Dunmead had only ventured as far as the upstairs parlour. Edward's attendance and condition, though having no improvement, for he mostly slept, was left chiefly to Mariah's care and attention. By the second morning, however, Elizabeth recovered herself enough to spend the afternoon with Edward, who regained some conscious minutes, enough to comprehend the seriousness of his condition. Later that day, Doctor Poole came to call on his patient; his report on Edward's condition was grim, and though all hope was not at an end, Elizabeth should at the very least prepare herself as he was not yet out of danger until the swelling had passed.

Many days were spent in this way. Barely a word was spoken between them all, as they were all anxious for him. Elizabeth was too fretful for anyone's company including her family, Mrs Dunmead took no wine, and Mariah and Aunt Mary were all silence.

It was little comfort when Edward was more awake and able to take more than wine, as food made him even more ill. The doctor then feared for his liver and spleen and prescribed a tonic that was to be given every four hours. Edward, however, became worse still. His pallor was sallow and clammy, his pulse hastened, and his delirium deteriorated.

Mariah and Aunt Mary went that Sunday morning to church for the service and to pray, while Elizabeth spent an affected teary morning at her husband's bedside. When they returned, Elizabeth was observed in the parlour drinking tea, Mariah joined her and following minute enquiries after her brother, took up a book in silence.

After several long minutes, Elizabeth could stand it no longer; she must speak up.

"I wonder that you can sit there reading." Elizabeth frowned and with a hiss added, "If I had brought about the near and most probable death of my brother, I would be distraught and in great despair." Mariah was aghast at her choice of words and surprised at being addressed so, she looked up from her book and suppressing a scoff, paused to catch her breath for something polite to say.

"And I am at a loss how you could possibly imagine that I revel in this tragedy. I might not faint at the first sign of calamity, but I can assure you, I feel these turn of events keenly, I am as anxious for his recovery as you could be." Mariah shook with the effort of composure. "But how am I in any way responsible for the accident, how do you account for such an accusation?" Elizabeth was taken aback by Mariah's tone, but with embittered sternness, persisted in her offensive accusations.

"Your vigil is admirable, but it is the work of a guilty conscience. If you were married, he would not need to attend business half so much. It is because of the burden of you that he has so few hours of repose." Mariah bit her lip with the effort of being silent. "Business that could be delayed at the very least."

"If you truly believe that to be the case, I pity you, because you will never understand Edward nor where his obligation truly lies…" Mariah shook her head.

"Oh, dear me, you overvalue your pity on me, but I think you do not understand me," replied Elizabeth sternly, "Let me be clear now… If Edward should die, and you are unmarried still, I will make sure that neither you nor your aunt see another penny of his money spent on either of you. You may imagine that he has provided for you in his will, but he has not, because we supposed that you would marry… But you have taken us for fools. And you may as well know now that the estate has neither entail nor jointure. I am to inherit everything, especially in my delicate situation." Elizabeth paused. "Now… if you should agree to marry before Edward dies, I will make you this promise that I will honour you your ten thousand pounds on your marriage and not a penny more. Of course, the longer you delay, the less it will become, keeping sisters who refuse to marry is so expensive, you know…" Elizabeth gave Mariah a perfunctory smile. "Perhaps now, you will reconsider your possibilities…" Mariah made no answer and Elizabeth, feeling she had triumphed at last, continued, "Mr Harward is a respectable man, and I have taken some pains to make excuses for you evading his attentions, but have a care, he is growing weary, I will not do so again." She paused and looked to the timepiece. "Mr Harward and his sister are to come for supper this evening, and I expect you will give him every attention. I, of course, will be watching. Though Miss Alexina and I have much to discuss, she has promised to tell me all about her new fashion from London."

"I see, how charming for us all," replied Mariah with all the politeness she could gather and she quit the room.

Mariah was in two minds about waiting on guests during Edward's recovery; for the effort of being diverting and charming company, but also that the business itself was a distraction from all that she felt on that score. She could not blame Elizabeth for wanting that relief, however privately she might choose to show angst, other people were not the same. Aunt Mary, however, could not so easily forgive Elizabeth for exposing them all so cruelly in their want of solitude for misery.

"Mr Harward, will you not carve for us all?" asked Elizabeth at dinner with a forced smile, "naturally, my dear Edward would have performed the duty," she paused, her voice thick with affected emotions. If he were not so frightfully taken ill." Elizabeth looked to Mariah for a moment, then added with a despondent air and stiff grimace, "But this will not do, we must be merry for our guests."

"Indeed, I shall, for I know of course he would… I am honoured by your request, it would be a pleasure, madam," replied Mr Harward.

"Excellent; of course, you must do so from where you are, sir," Elizabeth waved at the servant toward Mr Harward, "so that Mariah may observe how well you perform the duty at your own table."

Mariah hid behind her napkin, as she raised her eyebrows, and coolly replied, "You are mistaken, Elizabeth, I am not at all ignorant of Mr Harward's abilities. We have all observed, he carves very well," Mariah said smilingly. Mr Harward and Aunt Mary smiled.

"I particularly recall one evening, some pheasants that were in need of some skill for carving, and everyone said how beautifully he had done it," Elizabeth recalled and approved of Mariah's sentiments. Alexina, keen to have some play in the conversation, added her regret that it was before she had come, and would very much like pheasant at their next family dinner and she smiled at them all.

On Tuesday Mariah was grateful for the escape from Addison Terrace to attend a practice of the Grey's Musical Society, for, despite all the calamity around her, the Christmas performance was fast approaching. And she, quite overwrought with feelings, almost forgot her appointment with the Coburns' coach. Though she considered not attending, she was glad that she did, as she received many assurances of prayers and supplications for her brother. They were all so kind and understood that this was as much a balm of solace as her own prayers.

Later that week, Elizabeth retreated from waiting on any more guests, for they were all in a dread. The doctor was sent for again! Overnight, Edward developed an acute fever; his face was a greyish hue and his breath was faint. Mariah, exhausted from her previous duties to him, attended him still through grave expectations, as his wife was too weak with anxiety, and gave him water to drink and a towel for his face.

At length, the doctor had come with a diagnosis that was serious indeed, and the whole house felt it. Elizabeth's fresh understanding of her husband's condition and deterioration changed her attitude from avoidance to one of acceptance. Near death and all its foreboding emboldened Elizabeth to her sensibilities and her duty. She was determined in her new courage and firm in her conviction. Elizabeth sent for the

Reverend Green, dismissed Mariah from Edward's bedside, and took up the vigil herself.

It was a relief to Mariah that Elizabeth replaced her on two counts: her growing fatigue by her constant attendance to him day and night was overwhelming her own health, but also that she began to wonder if Elizabeth had any real feeling for her husband at all! Mariah was glad to learn, however, that Elizabeth's over-sensitive and delicate femininity had been too overcome, and not that she cared so little for his wellbeing, she could not formerly put herself out for his care.

Mariah's own feelings had become weary and weak from despair as she had been the sole responsibility of the sick until Elizabeth had discharged her. Aunt Mary, aware of her great-niece's present condition, suggested the following morning that she take the carriage for an airing, lest she too become ill; she had, after all, spent far too many days indoors.

Mariah thanked Aunt Mary for the suggestion but thought she would much prefer a walk. It was, after all, a fine day, and she felt emboldened to make the most of the last of the autumn sunshine. She intended to call on her friend Mrs Marsh, but with her thoughts mostly on her brother and none on her rising enervation; and without directing her steps, she found herself a mile or so away on the Oxford road. She was, however, only made acutely aware of where she was by the hallooing of a familiar voice.

"Miss Mariah? I thought it was you," he smiled. "Indeed, your beauty is unmistakable to me. But what a lucky chance! I was just on my way to you. I made the purchase of some music, of which, I very much hope, you will approve. See here," said Mr Harward, who was just about to open the papered package, when casting a second eye over his intended object of admiration, he observed the increasing fatigue of his companion. "Are you well, Miss Mariah?" asked he.

"Oh, quite well," lied she, discounting her faintness as being a little overheated on account of her walk. "I think I have walked farther than I intended," replied she smilingly.

"I would believe you if I had not the prior knowledge of your brother's condition. But as it is, I am sensible of all your exertions on that score, and if you were to take my advice, it would be to take a good day's rest, if not two. I am no doctor, of course. But truly, you look quite done for…" replied he and with that Mariah suddenly felt all her exhaustion at once and stumbled. Mr Harward held her steady and kindly suggested that she lean on him, as they walked in the direction of Partridge Lodge; which was barely a quarter mile.

Upon reaching Partridge Lodge, Mariah began to speak of her gratitude for his services and would he be so kind as to send for a carriage to take her home, but before she had spoken half so many words, Alexina Harward greeted them both and insisted that she take some refreshments with them, which were to be served directly, for Mariah looked positively famished, and said mostly to her brother that she saw it more as an obligation than a hospitable gesture.

"You are both very kind, but I must return home for news of Edward as soon as it comes." Mariah gulped back tears.

"Nay, please, I shall send my man and he shall bring you news; it would be most uncharitable of me to send you presently, for you really do look quite ill." Mariah, too tired to reason with them, relented at length and was seated by the fire in the most comfortable seating, and refreshments and tea were served. Mariah, however, barely touched her tea, for the chair really was very comfortable and she was asleep within several minutes.

That afternoon Aunt Mary was in receipt of two letters, one from Mr Harward explaining that Mariah was detained at Partridge Lodge on account of her sudden exhaustion and impromptu repose, but that every effort was being made to make her comfortable. The second letter was from Lady Coburn to inform both Mariah and Aunt Mary that her cousin Mr Probert and his wife were expected shortly in town and if they were up to being in company, they would be very welcome at Chifley Grey House.

***

Mariah awoke in an unfamiliar room, on a very comfortable and plush bed. She suspected the drawn curtains hid the setting sun and she sat up wondering how long she had slept; it must be several hours at least, for she really felt much better. Several moments later, a maid greeted her and wished her good morning.

"Oh, so it is not yet noon?" asked Mariah, confused.

"Noon, Mam?" replied the maid. "It is not yet seven." The maid promptly left the room, and Mariah was immediately at the window and slid back the curtain to reveal a new day. It both surprised and shocked her; how long had she slept? She noticed too that she was in bed clothes, and that her dress lay over a screen in the corner. She began to recall that she was at Partridge Lodge by the line of trees and shrubbery on the hill.

The maid returned with hot broth and tea, but before Mariah could object by a desire to get dressed, the maid added,

"Doctor's orders, Mam."

"He has been here?" asked Mariah, who ate immediately.

"Yes, Mam, you have been quite ill. He said that when you woke, I was to give you broth and sweet tea directly."

"How long have I been asleep? Oh, but how does my brother do? What news of him? I must go to him directly."

"Now Mam, you are on strict bed rest yourself. You are not well enough to go anywhere. But if you sit in bed and take your broth, I'll tell you directly."

"Very well," conceded Mariah, seeing argument was useless.

"It is Sunday morning, and the Master and his sister are on their way to church. I also have a letter here from your aunt. But the Master has advised me that I am to tell you there is very little change in your brother's condition; though his fever is a little less, he is no worse. Now… if you are well enough, you can join them for luncheon."

"Sunday you say, I do say I feel much better today, I must have slept for at least fourteen hours."

"It's nearer nineteen hours, mam."

"Oh," replied Mariah, finishing her broth. The maid gave her Aunt Mary's letter and quietly left the room.

The letter was much smaller than she anticipated, and she read the contents hoping for more detailed news of her brother; instead it contained a brief report on Edward's unchanged condition and a small note that she was not to exert herself too early lest she have a relapse and it wouldn't do to have two sick relatives! This surprised Mariah because though her Aunt Mary had never been so much as discouraging of Mr Harward, she had also not been encouraging either.

The maid returned at length and helped her dress and showed her to the drawing room downstairs, by a very warm fire.

"I have ordered a good luncheon today," declared Mr Harward to his sister and Mariah, when they returned. Mariah kindly thanked him; Alexina was all praise for her brother's thoughtfulness.

"You must be a good person, I think, and I should like to know you more," began Alexina when her brother left the room. "Eliza tells me regularly how sweet you are to herself and your brother. How much you have spared her feelings, by taking such good care of him. I spoke with your kindly Aunt Mary; we both of us expected you would want news of your brother—your Aunt Mary was so kind as to give me the latest this morning after the service. Though I doubt it will give you much comfort as he has not made any improvement at all. I'm deeply vexed to say it; I had hoped to give a favourable report, but it would not do, and on the contrary, it would most unkind to give you false hope."

"Oh yes, thank you. I understand," replied Mariah, "it is awkward to compose words at times like these, but there is no easy way to say someone's health is failing." Alexina nodded.

"Is not this nice?" asked Mr Harward when they were seated at table, a little while later.

"You are so kind to us all, Emmett," replied Alexina, "such a good luncheon, soup and partridge and every good thing, I can't imagine anything better."

"Oh, certainly this is a very fine luncheon, you have done very well, sir," replied Mariah with delicacy. Her thoughts so full of her brother, it was all she could do by way of a compliment and she hoped she would be spared the necessity of additional speeches in compliment of his table.

"If you are well enough after luncheon, Miss Mariah, I thought we might take a turn about the shrubberies; it is a very small park, and I did hope it would not be too strenuous to your health. But of course, if it is too much, we can admire the view from the upstairs gallery…"

"Thank you, I am sure a turn around the park will do me good. I had already determined to see the sun today." Both Mr Harward and his sister were most pleased. Mariah smiled politely and imagined that life with Mr Harward and his sister was not so deeply unpleasant as she had first thought. Though she did not love him, she hoped that she would at least be cared for; and now she only had to consider her Aunt Mary.

Mariah's growing anxiety for her inevitable situation, placed upon by her sister-in-law, was not wholly alleviated by the prospect of becoming Mrs Harward, but rather it relieved all anxiety for her Aunt Mary. Mariah practised smiling politely and prepared her mind for what she was certain would come. It was for Aunt Mary's ease and comfort that she considered very seriously Mr Harward's proposal, that came, while among the shrubberies, for she could not bear the thought of her aunt being reduced to a humble milkman's cottage on the other side of the river.

Mr Harward assured her in the sweetest adulations that he desired not only to relieve her of her spinsterhood but also, if Mariah would consent to be his wife, it would make him the happiest of men. In doing so, of course, he understood that it would also include her dear Aunt Mary, whom it would be an honour to welcome at Partridge Lodge. Mariah paused and looked away momentarily for courage and to put on her smile and nodded before looking upon his face. He looked most pleased with himself, with his success and rejoiced when they returned to the Lodge, in sharing the news with his sister. Alexina, anticipating the news, congratulated them both with enthusiasm and excitement.

Chapter Twelve

Mariah's initial assertions to her future spouse and sister that she was much better, was met with gentle dissuasion from travelling at present as she still looked too pale to be at all well. But Mariah would not be talked out of her acute desire to be home, to learn of the earliest news of her brother's condition, and begged to return home. If he would but lend her a carriage, it would be of little inconvenience to them both. Mr Harward, though a little anxious for Mariah's health, could not be so unfeeling and at length complied with her request and relieved his unease for her health by taking her thither himself.

On first reaching Addison Terrace, Mariah, eager to enquire after her brother's condition, was put off by Mr Harward's rapturous news. Upon seeing them all, he could not help but to make the announcement directly.

"My dear, dear friends, you see before you the happiest of men, for we are to be family: just this afternoon dearest Mariah has consented to be my wife."

"Sir, what excellent news!" cried Elizabeth, "Mama…? Aunt Mary, our dear Mariah is to be married at long last." Aunt Mary smiled politely, and Mrs Dunmead, who had been in the hall, was now nowhere to be seen. "Of course you need not concern yourselves with that which a brother might give in

place of a father. Such an old-fashioned business is it not…"
Elizabeth laughed. "Edward and I, of course, have been
expecting it for some time and he has given me leave to
approve the match."

"Oh, it is the best of news," added Alexina, "I am most
exceedingly pleased to be gaining a sister, at last; you cannot
think how tiresome it has been to have four brothers all my
life."

Mariah looked to her Aunt Mary for support, and though
Aunt Mary was subdued in her elation, for her voice and
manner were tolerably calm, her eyes showed more
apprehension then encouragement. But neither Mr Harward
nor Elizabeth paid Mariah or Aunt Mary any attention.

"Oh, but the banns!" Elizabeth smiled, "you must go
directly to see Reverend Green. What a pity it could not be
announced this morning… But of course, next Sunday will do
very well for a beginning. Of course, you must dine with us
this evening, if it is convenient." Mr Harward and his sister
were happy to oblige them all with their company.

When at last Mariah was free to speak plainly with her
aunt and see her sleeping brother for herself, she was relieved
to find that though he was not out of danger, his fever and
delirium had passed. Aunt Mary, of course, was silent for some
time before Mariah received any of her thoughts on the match.

"I know what it is you are doing," began Aunt Mary.

"Aunt… I…" Mariah started to protest, but a stern look
from her great-aunt silenced her in an instant.

"As I said, I know what you are about and your sacrifice
is admirable, but my dear girl, this is for life! And for someone
like you… so gifted in music and with all the sweetness and
gentleness in the world. You will be at the greatest

disadvantage in your future life. What can you be thinking? Can you not see how wretched it will be for you? And for myself? I, who must view it all in the greatest of torments, knowing you are grieved and neglected but worse still, for I will be powerless to change it. Can you not see, you are throwing yourself away on a man we know to be a gamester and insincere, and an even greater disadvantage for you; for it closes the prospect of a match with any other gentleman more than age… or situation. And a man such as he… He is far from the most suitable of matches. He has no restraint and his connexions are tenuous at best, though I will say he is attentive at present, I know it will not surprise you when I say he has a wandering eye, no woman could ever make him happy for long, and I am sure he could never make you so and more too, as he has no love of music," Aunt Mary added with almost a smile and looked away. "I am, however, perfectly serious in my assertions to you. I am old and I require but little to be comfortable, and I am sure, if we are in need of a change, we could spend time with my niece's family, the Milcrofts in Manchester, or Lady Forbes, for there are many rooms at Fornavis Priory." She paused, and though Mariah made no answer, she listened with all forbearance. "There is also another objection," added Aunt Mary suddenly, "As I truly believe, though others may not… all is not lost on his circumstance, though he is gravely ill, he is not yet dead and the severity of his illness wanes by the hour. And if he should live, Mariah… only think of what he should say on the match. For I am sure he is not of one mind as Elizabeth claims, and though you will think better of Elizabeth than she deserves, if what you tell me of your last conversation with Edward in Bostworth is true, we know she has lied at least once!"

"Well…" Mariah hesitated, "yes, that is true, but we will be reduced to less than two hundred pounds per annum, but Aunt Mary, though your reasons are accurate, it does not take into account what comfort can be got in solitude, what would you have me do? " asked Mariah thoughtfully.

"Write directly and apologise for raising his hopes, but that you must regrettably disappoint him forthwith. Of course, add a short courteous line of hopes that his disappointment will be of short duration!"

"I see. I will consider carefully your words, Aunt, but just now, I need some time of reflection. Another day will not prove ill for either of us," replied Mariah, frowning.

"No, that is true, but every day you delay, Elizabeth advances plans for your wedding."

***

As Aunt Mary had neglected to give Mariah the news in Lady Coburn's letter, Mariah learned of the Proberts' impending arrival at the practice on the Tuesday of the Grey's Musical Society. She was most pleased with the news, as she was eager to see Bridget again.

"It has been the work of many months' encouragement, I assure you," added Lady Coburn. "My cousin Charles Probert and his wife are to come to us on Friday fortnight and they are to stay for the Christmas duration."

"How charming," replied Mrs Norman.

"I look forward to seeing them on the Sunday following," added Mrs Green smilingly.

"I understand," continued Lady Coburn to Mariah, "you are not only acquainted, but you were also the means of bringing about the match when you were in London last summer?"

"Oh no, that is to say, we are acquainted… but to claim that I alone brought about the match… it is too much," disputed Mariah.

"You are overscrupulous, surely, they both speak highly of you… and what could they say of you but what I… we know of you already? You are so amiable and gracious, I defy anyone to speak ill of you." Mrs Norman nodded in agreement.

Mariah blushed and immediately thought of Elizabeth and was grateful that they, at least, had not heard her strictures on Mariah's faults. She then gave a brief account of the meeting at Vauxhall Gardens, careful to leave out any mischief on behalf of the Miss Fannings. Lady Coburn nodded her approval, Mrs Norman thought it charming and Mrs Green listened without interrupting once.

Later that week, Lady Coburn, distracted with preparations for her expected guests, did not attend the service on Sunday. Mariah had not spoken of her impending marriage at their practice on Tuesday, Mrs Norman was indisposed, and Mrs Green was late and presumed the news had been communicated and congratulations already given and happily received, before her tardy arrival.

The Proberts arrived and were received with pleasure at Chifley Grey House with their hostess still ignorant of Mariah's impending marriage. Mrs Norman, eager to meet the newcomers, was the first to call on them, the Saturday after the Proberts' arrival.

"Mrs Probert, how delightful to make your acquaintance. I hear you are as fond of our talented Mariah as we are. Is not her talent on the pianoforte the sweetest thing you have ever heard? Do you play and sing, Mrs Probert?" And without waiting for Brigitte to draw breath, Mrs Norman continued. "Oh but indeed, you must tell me your thoughts on the match, for it seems a curious connexion to me, and I have no doubt you will make it out far better than I, for your regard and understanding must have afforded you several weeks to adjust your ideas at least." Bridget shook her head in confusion.

"What match might that be, Mrs Norman?" added Lady Coburn, also puzzled by Mrs Norman's conversation.

"I presume you've heard that Mariah is to be married," added Mrs Norman. Lady Coburn looked astonished, Bridget regarded the news with confusion and Mr Probert, who had been standing by, admiring the view from the window, immediately turned around with a face as stunned as his hostess.

All in an uproar, her listeners cried out together. Mrs Norman was bewildered by their unified dismay and in astonishment and timidity repeated the news a second time.

"But surely you know that our dear Mariah is to marry Mr Harward at Christmas." Lady Coburn shook her head in utter amazement and mutely considered how it might be. But she could neither recollect any communication of the kind nor recall any behaviour that alluded to a particular attachment. More surprised was she that Mariah had not spoken of it on Tuesday last, and she looked to Bridget to see how she bore it. Her curiosity was awakened, however, by the thoughtful look and manner which, of course, was more of disappointment than disbelief.

Mrs Norman continued, "I am surprised, it is all her family talk about; they have been planning the union since he first come to the neighbourhood. How do you account for never having heard it?" Again Lady Coburn was at a loss for a reply.

After Mrs Norman had taken her leave, Lady Coburn waited in agonising patience for herself and Bridget to be alone in the drawing room. Sir Arthur, after several well-meaning looks, careful suggestions, and at length, bold hints by his wife, suggested that Mr Probert might like to see his plans for the new mill in Southfield.

"Now, Mrs Pr…"

"Oh please, call me Bridget."

"Thank you… Now, Bridget, I hope you will not think it an imprudence, but I must say your look of confusion did not escape my notice when we all heard the news of a marriage that seemed remarkably strange to the rest of us, even to Mrs Norman. And as Mariah has long been a favourite in this house, it both grieves me and pleases me, for it shows a sincere concern for our dear Mariah, that I have no doubt you share with me, so I will be open with you and hope that you feel you can return the favour."

Bridget sighed with relief. "I am so pleased you share my reservations on the match," replied she.

"Indeed, I do, but I fear I may also be to blame," returned Lady Coburn.

"Oh no, Mariah has always spoken so highly of you, I am sure that cannot be true."

"And I likewise of her, Mariah has always been in special regard because I have always hoped, though I have never spoken it for fear it would be injurious to my hopes, you understand… It is my desire that she would one day be my sister." Bridget was surprised but made no answer. "But it seems now the foolish dreams of an older sister. They always got along so well in their youth, and though they have only resumed a familiar acquaintance in the last twelvemonth, as Frederick has been away, perhaps she does not desire him as well as she once did... I know Frederick too admires... admired her more highly than any other woman, but perhaps he too has changed his mind." Bridget shook her head with increasing deliberation; she had to speak directly, and it was only sincere distress that would cause her to speak so boldly and interrupt Lady Coburn.

"Oh no, no, that's not true, I know Mariah was steadily against any connexion of the kind." Lady Coburn was taken aback. "Forgive me," continued Bridget, "but I must speak plainly." She then related some part of the conversation the two of them had shared on well-meaning relatives and their opinions and that she truly believed that Mariah admired her Frederick still. "But I believe," continued Bridget, "it was your uncle who dashed her hopes entirely..." Bridget blushed in dismay at speaking ill of her husband's relations. "Forgive me for speaking ill of Sir Niels just now, I am sure he had his reasons..." Lady Coburn, though shocked and several moments silent, then appealed to Bridget to tell her the whole story at once. Here, however, she could not be gratified, as Bridget only discerned that after Sir Niels's speech, Mariah had all but given up hope of a nearer connexion with Frederick and that she, Mariah, truly felt herself to be divided from Frederick forever.

Astonishment was not over and Lady Coburn's alarm increased when she heard of how he had spoken to Mariah, as Bridget confessed her own opinion that she understood that Sir Neils had been severe upon their friend. Lady Coburn made up her mind and instantly resolved to write to her uncle that very day.

Later that night, Mr Probert overheard the whole and was sorry for Mariah, and though he knew his cousin Frederick to be most exceedingly attached, he kept his own counsel on the feelings of others.

***

After many agonising attempts and discarded sheets of ivory paper, Lady Coburn penned a letter to her uncle, to enquire for the particulars of his dealings with Mariah and her family last summer, as she felt sure that Mariah had been wronged in some way. She did not dare to hope that he would send an early reply, for a less important man would consider the request beneath his notice, though it was from a favoured niece; and she hoped that a fortnight would be sufficient time to bring a response. Every day delayed was a day nearer to the marriage of her friend. Lady Coburn, however, would not broach the subject with her friend till she was in receipt of a reply, and every day she delayed was a distressing hardship which she shared with Bridget alone.

Chapter Thirteen

By the second Sunday that the marriage banns were read, Elizabeth began to feel secure in her hopes of soon having Addison Terrace all to herself. Her elation extended to Mr Harward and his sister, who were frequent guests, and she relished the soon to be successful match at every opportunity to triumph over Mariah, save one. That was her delicate rebuttals to admit Edward's imminent decline.

Mariah was surprised to find, on numerous occasions, her admittance to Edward's sick chamber prevented by way of Elizabeth's attendance or a locked door.

"Oh dear me no, he has just taken his rest tonic," replied Elizabeth when Mariah approached Edward's room for the second time that day. "Besides, the doctor said he is very weak, and I should limit his visitors, lest the strain claim his life… earlier… you understand… And I am sure that we are both anxious to give him as long as possible. Surely you would not wish to cause him pain." Mariah conceded that she would not and returned to the drawing room with her aunt.

"I do not see why I should be prevented from seeing a brother before he dies," said Mariah quietly to her aunt after another thwarted attempt to see him that afternoon.

"No, nor I," agreed Aunt Mary.

"We know him to be so very ill, and I am just as capable of being as quiet and gentle as she...." Mariah paused thoughtfully and looked to her aunt for encouragement in her hopes. "But what is your own view on her behaviour?"

"My own view? I confess I am surprised you ask! You give me leave to have an opinion on your brother's health? Yet refuse my views on other matters." Aunt Mary shook her head. Mariah was silenced for several moments... She was not prepared to discuss her forthcoming marriage to Mr Harward just now and returned the conversation to that of Elizabeth's schemes.

"But of this new arrangement, though? Preventing my seeing Edward, or you. Is it so imperative for his health to have no visitor other than his wife...? And yet his condition is not worse, for the doctor comes less often... Or is it because he has no hope...! What other reasons can she have?" suggested Mariah tearfully to her aunt. Aunt Mary sighed and shook her head.

"Hmm, you still think better of her than she deserves. But I will say this, whatever her reasons, you can be sure they are of a selfish nature."

"Oh Aunt, surely a husband is more important than petty schemes, she must really feel his imminent loss."

"Ha! Yes, she feels it uncommonly well, but not as you believe, I am convinced there is some other reason and you can be sure it is for her own gain. I tell you now, prepare yourself for something quite shocking. I believe Edward might not be as ill as he was once thought to be."

***

Sir Niels, being in receipt of his niece's letter, deemed it a most strange request for information he had long assumed she was already in a position of understanding for many months, if not years; for they lived in the same town for more than a decade. He gave it every attention the morning of its arrival in hopes of relieving his curiosity directly.

Hans Place, London

My Dear Niece,

I received your letter this morning and I was astonished you ask about something so trivial. What has happened to cause you so much alarm! Felicity, you have written in such haste and concern for someone so far beneath you. What powers of persuasion has this ward to vex all my relations! I never imagined that my niece had been deceived as well as my nephew. I cannot understand how you are ignorant that she is the ward of your friend Edward and his wife and has been much trouble to them that I must conclude you to be painfully deceived. Let me relieve your mind now and share with you the true facts, so you too can be rid of this fraudulent charlatan.

I had the good fortune to meet with your friend Edward and his new bride last summer when they were in London, and I soon learned how fortuitous it was to be well met. Not long after our meeting, she confessed to me her surprise that I had not only invited the ward of her husband but had allowed someone with such low connexions and wholly without class or distinction to spend so much time with my nephew. I was immediately perplexed at having been so deceived myself and I resolved to let the ward know my sentiments as soon as she was alone. You can imagine how seriously I treated this intelligence and how swiftly I acted. My annoyance only grew when I found Frederick to be taken in so much as to be deceived in love. And I believe it was almost too late; the separation from this ward of your friend has been a trial for Frederick. But I trust in time he will find another worthy of him.

I am sorry to give you pain, dear Felicity, but I would rather you know of your mistake at once than you be deceived another moment by the snare of falsehoods this ward has created.

Your attentive uncle.

Lady Coburn, on receiving his reply, was all vexation and despair, her mind so full of the injustice and her heart instantly heavy with the sorrow she felt for Mariah's cause. Her distress was so great, she shook with the effort to compose herself and drew the notice of her guests. Bridget was immediately by her side. In truth, the contents of his reply rendered her speechless for so many minutes together that she thrust the letter into Bridget's hand for her to read aloud.

The whole house knew at once, as Lady Coburn did, that this was a gross falsehood, that Mariah's relation to her brother had never been in question and knew her to be Edward's true and full sibling.

After a good half hour to think and compose herself, Lady Coburn's vexation gradually transformed from horror to anger, from shock to disdain at Elizabeth's betrayal, lies and total want of propriety and thoughtfulness. Consideration immediately then changed from hatred for Elizabeth to despair for Mariah's feelings.

"How could she bear it," said Lady Coburn at length. "What misery she must be feeling. And what must she think of me…" She dabbed at her eyes. "Oh, and my uncle, my poor uncle has been vilified and wronged by such vexatious cruelty, what wretchedness, what wickedness."

"It was very hard at first, but she accepted it in time as beyond her circumstance..." replied Bridget to ease Lady Coburn's concerns.

"Yes, that is shamefully obvious... or she would never have accepted the advances of another...." She paused, then added, "No matter which way I think of her being betrothed to anyone other than Frederick, I keenly feel her to be painfully wronged. We must make it right, Mariah must know her triumph and Elizabeth must know her place. But will you come with me? I am sure she must justly hate me? And I feel weak at the thought of confronting her, but it must be put right... today. Not a moment to lose."

Lady Coburn had always governed herself with a calmness that was a steady influence on those around her, without rashness or loud tempers, but even she was distracted by haste. Her desire to make right at once all the lies Elizabeth had set against Mariah's character. She rang the bell to have the carriage made up directly. Sir Arthur, however, quickly interrupted their plans and suggested an alternate course of action. If Lady Coburn and Bridget would but put off their trip for a quarter hour, there might be time enough to send a letter by her uncle and perhaps make the ten o'clock mail coach to London. This was decidedly better, and their little trip was deferred. She ignored her uncle's criticisms on hurried letters and jotted down her correspondence as quickly as her thoughts would permit for reason and sensibility. The letter was addressed and sealed; Mr Probert himself offered to take the letter to post by horse and was just in time without a second to lose for the London Mail Coach.

Lady Coburn knew her uncle, Sir Niels, was not unfeeling or unscrupulous, and therefore moderately approachable on suppositions that appeared fixed in the minds of others. She, therefore, dared to hope that her uncle's mind would be changed once he knew the truth of it.

***

The days grew shorter, and Mariah's impending marriage to Mr Harward began to burden her mind with difficulties. Each time her anxieties attempted to overwhelm her, she reminded herself of her duty to her aunt and the financial advantage to them both. Mariah was also conscious that liberties to visit whom she wished once married, and the discretion to visit all in her acquaintance, might be changed. She called on Mrs Marsh. But it was the wrong place to visit. Mrs Marsh was all elation at the discovery of her friend's engagement. She spoke endlessly of her raptures at the announcement, her delight at her friend's choice of husband, and only added twice in ten minutes that she always knew it would come right in the end.

A quarter hour's visit was all Mariah could bear; while she herself despaired at the closeness of the wedding, being only a fortnight and a day off, it was too much to be continually reminded of that which she struggled to accept as her own fate. She did not, however, return home directly; she walked in the direction of St Laurence's and the gardens beyond by way of distraction and was relieved not to meet with anyone before she returned home to the news that she had missed Lady Coburn's and Mrs Probert's visit. Her anxiety only increased by the acknowledgement that Lady Coburn and Bridget must also be acquainted with the news. It was a torment to join

151

Elizabeth and Aunt Mary for tea in the upstairs parlour that evening with anything but a well-rehearsed smile. She was grateful that the Harwards had not joined them that day and excused herself when Elizabeth began speaking of wedding plans.

She wished she could stay in the privacy of her own room forever, and with nostalgic lamentation admired anew the walls, furnishings and the comfort of her own room.

The following day, Mariah remained indoors all morning, till a carriage arrived and Lady Coburn alighted. Elizabeth, not prepared for Lady Coburn's second visit in as many days, dared not withhold numerous pleasantries or extension of courtesy of refreshment, offered much with little success. Though still hotly fierce in her disgust for Elizabeth's conduct and impropriety, Lady Coburn was all politeness.

"I thank you, no," said she at length with a cursory smile, "Though I too have much to say, if you would but show me to where Mariah is presently, it will relieve us both from speaking needlessly."

"Mariah?" Elizabeth replied, "What has she to do about it? I am the Lady of this house; communications of import must go through myself alone."

"But of course, if it is the business of the house, which it is not," replied Lady Coburn. Elizabeth was taken aback and at a complete loss for a reply, 'til a maid stepped forward to show Lady Coburn to Mariah's room. Elizabeth made no answer.

Mariah saw her arrive from an upstairs window and trembled in fright. What could she have to say? She must know of her uncle's accurate suppositions and disgust at the connexion. She prepared herself for visitors at once. There was a knock on the door, Lady Coburn entered and the door was closed behind her.

"Oh, Lady Coburn, you must allow me to apologise, please…"

"I will do no such thing. Oh, my dear Mariah, no indeed, It is I who must begin with apologies. I am, I am exceedingly sorry to be so abrupt with you but you must hear me first, for then neither of us will waste time on needless emotions and tears." She sat down by Mariah and began with Elizabeth's treachery and vulgar lies to her conscientious uncle and that she was convinced once he learned the truth of it, he would welcome Mariah all the more, especially once he learned of Lady Coburn's own desire to call her sister, which was matched by several other members of the family. Mariah blushed and blushed again while her emotions overwhelmed her.

"But are you certain this is how it is? Surely this is vanity," replied she, "and what does your brother know of this? Surely he has forgotten me now he is engaged, if not married to Miss Harper." Lady Coburn shook her head slowly and assured her that her brother was not engaged to anyone. When Mariah's tears had subsided and she acknowledged all that Lady Coburn had said as truth, she began to ponder at her own fate. She suddenly wished to be free of her engagement to Mr Harward. Lady Coburn, elated at Mariah's conclusions, could not be more willing to hurry her letter than by offering to send it by her own footman directly.

Later that morning, it then followed that Aunt Mary, keen to hear how their Christmas performance of the Grey's Musical Society was improving, was invited by Lady Coburn and gratefully accepted by Aunt Mary to join them for practice and tea. Away from Elizabeth, and the chance of being overheard, the conversation naturally flowed to Mariah's present situation. Aunt Mary, wholly unaware of the recent development, praised Lady Coburn for her influence and success to achieve what she could not. Aunt Mary was soon apprised of the whole story, who almost laughed at their serious faces.

"Why!" began Aunt Mary. "It is barely a fortnight ago I shared with Mariah that Elizabeth had some wickedness afoot for her own gain, was it not, Mariah?" Mariah nodded; Aunt Mary scoffed in spite of herself and continued. "Ward indeed!! There is, however, a ward in this story." Aunt Mary looked to each of them in turn and nodded. "And as I can see the secrets of Mrs Dunmead are damaging to the reputation of others… well, perhaps if I too had been unscrupulous and mercenary, more than one undesirable marriage might have been avoided, but what is done is done!"

"What secrets has Mrs Dunmead? Is not she merely the unfortunate widow of a late husband in trade?" asked Lady Coburn. "What secret has she other than that? Though not favourable amongst gentry, it is an honest living."

"No, though I see you have noticed as I have that she has thrown off her widow's garb and with it any associations to trade." Lady Coburn nodded.

"You do tease us all, Aunt Mary. I have heard this before," added Mariah with a kind smile.

"Nay, for your sake," replied Aunt Mary, eyeing her niece with a caring smile, "I think it is time. It is better to bring secrets into the light when they are used ill. It is the best recipe I know for reducing that which is puffed up like a red robin, to its rightful order. Though it is a very great scandal! And I hope not too offensive for your hearing, Lady Coburn. For it is my hope and also my justification that it will amend Mariah's reputation and respectability and secure your uncle's favour." Lady Coburn was willing to make an exception and all three ladies listened intently.

"My brother John made the acquaintance of a young Mr Dunmead, fresh from an education in finance, and like many young men, determined to be better than his father. And by all that he said and did, very unlike his father he was, for he had a charitable heart, he was all friendliness and eager to please. He would sometimes stay with my family at Southampton in summer. Years later, I learned that he had done well for himself in trade and had taken up with a young lady from Newcastle and for some time we were out of contact. Many years later John told me he had lost them both in childbirth. In later years, while my brother was alive, he would often dine with us if he was by, but he made it very clear, he had no mind to marry again. That was until he met a young lady who on noticing she had caught his eye, was very persuasive. I know not how she came to be with child, but he took it upon himself to relieve her imminent disgrace. She, of course, agreed to his inclination, if he would but marry her forthwith. So they wed… she had a daughter and he agreed to provide for her daughter; after a few years, however, they had another daughter of their own before he became ill, and to this second daughter he left everything else."

"Are you saying that the first daughter is Elizabeth?" asked Mariah. Aunt Mary agreed that it was. Understanding blossomed over their faces.

Mariah would need at least a day to contemplate this new information but as Musical Practice was about to commence, she had to defer her contemplation and feelings till the evening, in the solitude of her room.

It was clear to Mariah that she had misjudged Elizabeth's motives. She had never thought anyone admitted to her family could behave so cruelly and without regret. She began to question everything she had doubted about Aunt Mary's suppositions. All this time, Aunt Mary had been acutely accurate of Elizabeth's motives which had been, Mariah supposed, ones of jealousy and resentment. She had thought too well of Elizabeth, and perhaps even the guidance of many who had encouraged her to attach herself to Mr Harward. She had yielded too readily to their wishes without consideration for her own feelings. And more too was the sting that she had continually resisted the opinions of those closest; those whom she treasured most had been least considered. What needless anguish she had suffered in discounting their counsel! What was also clear was if Elizabeth had one ounce of her step-father's charitable kindness, this secret might never have come to light, but now the responsibility must rest in its proper place.

Mariah had spent most of the following day in her room and was relieved when summoned to dinner that evening that it was a small party gathered at table; without Edward or the Harwards, meals were often eaten in silence.

"I must apologise to you, Mariah," said Elizabeth at length. Mariah, a little startled by such a beginning, looked to Aunt Mary in earnest.

"Pardon?" answered Mariah, hoping she had misheard.

"No need for alarm, I only meant to apologise on Mr Harward's behalf; I am sure he is well, he is just indisposed this evening, and cannot join us for a family dinner," added Elizabeth. Mrs Dunmead laughed. "And why is that amusing?" Mrs Dunmead made no answer and returned her attentions to her soup. Elizabeth shook her head and the meal continued in silence.

Chapter Fourteen

The following day it was in general circulation within a half hour of breakfast, that Mr Harward and Mrs Dunmead was engaged to be married directly. The news was frightfully scandalous to some and was met with many doubtful looks and sneering suspicions.

When the news reached Elizabeth, the whole house heard her violent shrieks of alarm; Mariah knew Elizabeth would seek her out at once and prepared herself for the barrage of questions she knew must follow. Aunt Mary immediately took up some knitting beside her in the downstairs parlour.

Elizabeth seethed from one end of the house to the other, hunting where Mariah might be and had almost concluded her out of doors when she chanced upon her in the downstairs parlour by the windows. Elizabeth halted, and eyed them suspiciously, for Mariah, especially, seemed remarkably composed for someone who was now by all accounts unattached.

"Here you are! Now.. my dear, come with me, we must speak alone together." Elizabeth waited over long for Mariah, who looked up and smiled but remained where she was seated. In heightened anticipation and anxiety Elizabeth persisted. "I beg your pardon… did you not hear me just now, we have much to discuss and I am certain your aunt would not wish to tire herself, nor anyone else, listening to all when I know you would prefer to excite anticipation with expected felicity at the happy event.”

“But I have no wish to.” Mariah looked up from her fine stitches and smiled politely, shaking her head. Elizabeth’s face showed her displeasure. “You are not my patron, nor am I in your employ to warrant any unpleasant one to one speeches. What you have to say can be said here, in the open.”

“Very well,” paused Elizabeth, taking a seat. She gave them both the news which had been circulating that morning, every moment her voice growing more discordant, and shrill; and at length demanded an explanation, for she was sure it was the grossest falsehood, which she suspected Mariah herself had put about. For several moments Mariah was silent; she pondered what she might say first. “WELL?” Elizabeth shrieked in frustration!

“I suppose I might answer you your questions, but I have several of my own that ought to negate yours.” Elizabeth looked from Aunt Mary to Mariah with raised eyebrows. “It is a mystery to me why a newly married woman has been persistently eager to cause strife betwixt her husband and his sister, his aunt, his cousins, and all those in his acquaintance from the eve of her wedding ’til long after the honeymoon.”

“And I cannot fathom why you think it is acceptable to be a burden to your relations all your life,” replied Elizabeth. Aunt Mary scoffed; Mariah ignored this statement entirely.

“It had not been a month after your honeymoon before you set in motion your poison to the uncle of a family, well connected with me and many others.” Elizabeth blushed.

"Nonsense!! This is all in the past. This does not explain Mr Harward's supposed engagement to my mother."

"But of course, it does, because that uncle, Sir Niels… Lady Coburn's uncle… now knows precisely what you have enacted against me, and they are all vastly disgusted. They will forgive Edward by and by, though it is unlikely you will ever be tolerated in their company again nor all those in his influence." Elizabeth grew pale.

"You will get nothing!" hissed Elizabeth. "Nothing! I will follow through with my promise, and as of next week, I will see to it directly that Addison Terrace will no longer be home for either of you." There was a loud crash behind them; greatly startled, they all turned at once to see Edward limping through the door, using a cane to both get their attention and steady his gait. Mariah leapt from her chair and embraced him with tears. He smiled and nodded and looked to Aunt Mary who was slightly teary. She was relieved to see her great-nephew regain his strength and voice.

"My sister and aunt are not going anywhere!" said he gravely, then added in a softer tone, "And the only way my sister would get nothing… would be if she married that Harward gamester."

"Oh, my dear, you are too unwell to be up, you don't know what you are saying…" cooed Elizabeth, but Edward pushed her away.

"Enough!" continued Edward sternly. "It is evidently apparent that you cannot be trusted with an ounce of kindness to anyone; save your own selfish interests. You leave me with no choice other than to see to it that you are no longer to give orders in this house, and furthermore you are never to speak for me again!" Elizabeth momentarily stared from Mariah to

Edward without daring to look at Aunt Mary. She then turned away and hastily left the room.

It was not long before the news of the new impending marriage was all about town. By the Sunday the news of Mrs Dunmead's reputation and marriage overshadowed Mariah's engagement and the whole town forgot Mariah had ever been betrothed at all.

It was poor consolation for Elizabeth, whose agitation at the lost expense of one wedding, that she sullenly agreed to transfer arrangements, which could not be annulled for Mariah's nuptials, to that of her mother's.

By the following week, the news of the new engagement was followed by several whispers of Mrs Dunmead's former reputation; the natural assumption then moved from her past to Mr Harward's depravity, and half the town turned on him in disgust.

The next week, Mariah returned from musical practice to find herself alone; Edward, desiring to be out of doors despite the gusty wind, called on the Matlocks, with Aunt Mary encouraged and his wife compelled to join him. But her solitude was soon interrupted by the calling of an unwelcome visitor. Without admittance, the maid informed Mariah that Mr Harward had called and wished to speak with her. Mariah, surprised by his nerve, advised the maid to turn him away, but she soon returned saying that he would not go until he had seen her. Mariah knew very well that there was nothing else to do except speak with him.

"Miss Mariah…" began he, speaking loudly over the winds, as neither the maid nor Mariah had allowed him to cross the threshold, "Please allow me to apologise for all the rumours, I never meant to draw you into scandal nor tarnish your reputation, you are too kind for all the world in general and I beg you will reconsider us. Nothing has made me happier… for many months than the expectation of being with you for life. You alone make me happy, and I am convinced that no one else can make you so." He then took a step closer and added, "Are we not formed for each other… Indeed, I do not think two people are more suited than…"

"Pardon me, Mr Harward," Mariah interrupted, taking a step back. "These apologies, as you call them, are not necessary, for it is not I that is besmirched; and your speeches are wasted on me… Such inconstancy is not the behaviour of a gentleman, nor will it win any favour with me." Her eyes narrowed in discouragement. His face showed his struggle for speech but made no answer. "Nay, indeed, sir, you may give your reasons to the winds and you may fare better with her than you ever will with me. You will talk and she will bite, and if that is all that you endure, it will be well for you." She then turned and went hastily away, determined not to endure another second of his company, and the maid hastily closed the door behind her.

***

A week before Christmas, the Grey's Musical Society performed its Christmas Concert at Chifley Grey House. The guests were welcomed and seated. Mariah and the other ladies waited in another room while the guests arrived. Mariah clenched her fingers together tightly and paced the room. She considered who the guests might be, would Mr Tenby be amongst them, and she almost smiled to herself, and then recalled that the uncle too might attend and she twisted her hands again in agitation.

"Come now," said Mrs Norman to Mariah as they waited, "you look utterly overwrought, is it not generally my domain, yet I am composed and calm, as you see; is everything all right?" But before Mariah could answer, Mrs Green hurriedly entered the room from the parlour.

"Here's some pretty news for you," said Mrs Green pausing to catch her breath. "Mrs Marsh has had a baby girl, and she is perfectly formed."

"Oh, wonderful!" exclaimed Mariah, distracted from her own thoughts and delighted at the news; she then immediately enquired and was assured that both mother and child were the picture of health.

The time for recital arrived, and they all took their places. The pieces played were performed beautifully, pleasant and graceful, Mrs Norman only hit two wrong notes, and Mrs Green sang everything in tune.

It was not until after the performance that Mariah noticed one who had been the cause of much anxiety; though he did not immediately approach her. He was usurped by Bridget, who was one of the first to personally congratulate her on their performance.

"I hear too, your brother has made a remarkable recovery, is he much better?" said she; Mariah nodded smilingly, and agreed that he was, that he was walking and had been out twice this week. "What a blessed relief for your family to have him restored!" added Bridget kindly. Mariah could not agree more readily or wholeheartedly. Bridget nodded, then added, "I am so glad to have come to Reading. Charles and I would have come sooner, but he had some business in town that could not be avoided. I am, however, exceedingly relieved we arrived no later."

"Oh," Mariah gasped, "say nothing of that," she continued, with a sigh, and the next moment she was all captivation in another direction.

"Oh no, but indeed, so much has happened in this week alone, I can scarcely take it in… Oh by the by, Lady Coburn has given me leave to invite you to come to dinner tomorrow evening, if it is convenient?"

"Pardon?" Mariah answered. It was evident she had not paid attention to her friend's words. Bridget cast her eye to see who had caught Mariah's attention and smiled.

"Oh, I believe… Lady Coburn needs my assistance…" added Bridget hastily.

"No no, you must stay…" Mariah whispered and grasped her arm to stop her from walking away. Mariah's alarm was heightened as Mr Tenby approached and Bridget, whose arm was held fast, relented.

"I must thank you for all your dedication," said Mr Tenby, acknowledging them both. "I hear that you all practised intensely for today; it was very well done, but also too for all your kindness to my sister in her constant determination." He then added with a grin, "I am sure she is a ruthless tyrant in pursuit of perfection." Mariah laughed, Bridget only smiled. Mr Tenby then enquired after her family with particular consideration for her brother's health.

"I really must go and assist Lady Coburn." Bridget looked to Mariah, who nodded. She then excused herself and left Mariah with Mr Tenby.

"But really, it was a sweet performance," said Mr Tenby again. "Very well done by you all…"

"Thank you," answered Mariah.

"… My sister is to have a family party tomorrow, I understand you are to join us?" Mariah said that she was. "I am pleased, what a pleasant addition it will be."

"Certainly, I have grown quite partial to family dinners at Chifley Grey House," replied Mariah with a grin.

"Indeed yes… My sister is very fond of hosting them…But, Miss Mariah…" Mr Tenby shook his head. "You must allow me to say I am very sorry for all that has happened; your forbearance is to be admired. I must apologise for all the grief and mortification it has cost you."

"Not at all, it was not of your making, so you have nothing to apologise for…"

"Though you do blame my uncle," answered he.

"No, how was he to know, and really, if it had really been as she described, would he not be justified in his guarded defence of all he holds dear?" Mr Tenby nodded; he had not considered it in such a way as she had till now, and he admired her all the more for her forgiveness and kindness to his uncle, where many would have condemned and held highly blameable for a twelvemonth. How just was her heart, how sweet was her temper. "And you… are you well, how was your journey from London and Lancashire to Sussex, I hear?"

Mr Tenby laughed. "Exceedingly dull, I can assure you, without a companion in the world!"

"How dreadful… and how did you occupy your time in the evenings? Were you forced to play endless cards and backgammon?" asked Mariah teasingly. Mr Tenby admitted while attempting not to smile that he was obliged to do the latter a little more than was pleasant and spent much time reading and writing letters.

∗∗∗

The following evening at Chifley Grey House Mariah arrived a little early to dinner at Lady Coburn's request and was led to the drawing room. Mariah halted when the door was opened and standing before her was Sir Niels.

"My uncle," said Lady Coburn, "arrived this morning. It is his wish to be more acquainted with you and your family." Sir Niels nodded and invited Mariah to take a seat while he himself did not. He remained standing for the whole of his palpable apology. Mariah truly felt it to be too much, and she had long forgiven him already. When he was finished, she shared with him her own thoughts, that he ought to be absolutely pardoned, considering really, he had only acted out of consideration of a niece and nephew that he undoubtedly loved, and that really it ought to be credited to him as a proof of character as he had acted in a difficult situation, however unwelcome, for the benefit to his nephew. Sir Niels smiled at them both, and thought of Mariah more highly than he had hoped and with a sudden twinkle in his eye, greatly desired to be congratulating Frederick on a nearer connexion soon.

The dinner was a pleasant party and Mariah especially was grateful that no partridge was served.

∗∗∗

Mariah's spirit was light; the blessedness of relief and happiness lasted several days when she suddenly remembered her friend Mrs Marsh and arranged to call on her as soon as may be.

Her plans, however, were delayed when news reached them on the Monday before Mrs Dunmead's wedding that her groom had gone missing. Upon further investigation by Edward and his Uncle John, Partridge Lodge was not only without its chief occupant, but the report from the gardener was that Mr Harward and his sister had left at first light on Monday. The gardener was applied to for further information and when asked if he had any idea of Mr Harward's plans or direction, the gardener only commented that he thought it odd that Mr Harward had packed everything himself and had suspected that he was returning to his family in Brighton.

Mr Marsh was then applied to and confirmed that Mr Harward himself had spoken of family at Brighton, but that he had only met him whilst in London and had never actually met any of his family other than those who had come to Reading.

It was, therefore, the general consensus that Mr Harward and his sister had travelled south. Mr Matlock, feeling it too much for Edward to ride so far so soon, took it upon himself to join Mr Marsh to go as far as Farnborough. Upon their return, the news was not favourable. No sighting of them had been made.

By the end of the week, Mariah, the whole house and half the neighbours discovered through another acrimonious fracas between Elizabeth and Mrs Dunmead that the lease on Partridge Lodge was three months in arrears. Elizabeth then continued her fierce censure with her husband; that if he had not interfered, her mother's expenses would not be reduced by the loss of income from Partridge Lodge, and by extension he had done Mr Harward wrong. For he had been left so desperate without ten thousand pounds on his marriage. Adding to the scandal, it was soon heard, all over town, that Mr Harward, as charming as he was, had left many debts.

Mariah and Aunt Mary could hardly help overhearing it all. Aunt Mary pondered in amusement if Elizabeth and Mr Harward had acted by design; he to pay his debts and she to gain the freedom of the house. Mariah listened to Aunt Mary with no small amount of alarm and agreed that while it was plausible, Elizabeth would surely never admit it and Mariah was made more thankful that she was free of the connexion.

Mariah then desired to be out of doors and away from hostilities and resolved to call on Mrs Marsh.

"Ooh, my dear one. Please, please forgive me," said Mrs Marsh close to tears, "…for my interference, my encouragement to you last spring to give him a second chance. It is unforgivable! Had we known… You must believe me when I tell you that neither I nor Mr M had any idea he was so very immoral. It is very wicked of him, and Mr M, now… even now regrets the acquaintance and the introduction, for it was he that introduced you last May."

"Oh, Roberta," Mariah replied and embraced her friend. "It is all forgot." Roberta looked aghast. "You mistake me, I am disappointed that my extended family is included in the disgrace, but I am not wounded."

"You're not?" Roberta dried her eyes.

"No, I have never really considered him at all, engagement or no."

"But you said your feelings surprised you, that you don't know how you could have missed it before. Those were your words last summer, I perfectly recall at the public ball in June, just before you went to London."

"Oh… no." Mariah smiled and recalled dancing with Mr Tenby. "I wasn't thinking of Mr Harward…."

"Then who?" asked Roberta with incredulity. She was beyond shocked at her friend's confession. "You have been very sly. Tell me at once who you have grown to admire these six months."

"Mr Tenby…" said Mariah with such affected happiness in her eyes that she could hardly be doubted.

"Lady Coburn's brother? But have you any idea of his feelings?" asked Mrs Marsh. "Not that I would now be contrary, after my constant encouragements to you formerly. But really, here I must caution you, dear Mariah." Mariah made no answer and Roberta continued. "You know I would never wish to affront either of you, but you must consider that the disadvantage reduces your chances of success… that is to say—I know you would not wish to injure the special regard you enjoy with his family." Roberta looked hurt and her agitation increased with Mariah's continued silence. "She has always been generous with us, especially you, I think…"

"You are determined… you mean to dissuade me then…" replied Mariah, trying not to smile.

"Perhaps I do… Does Lady Coburn know of this?" Mariah nodded, and still tried not to smile but was at every moment being provoked to do so. "And there is yet another objection, which you forget, I think… What of his feelings, is he not engaged?" Mariah shook her head. She paused on what to say, for she wished to preserve what little of good reputation Elizabeth had left and preserve Sir Niels's character entirely. At length, she explained with delicacy, that it was an odd case of mistaken identity. Mrs Marsh looked at her friend with apprehensive curiosity and wonder.

"Is it really true? It seems a remarkably happy and advantageous circumstance. But of course it must be true; Lady Coburn, of course, knows what her own brother is about." Roberta then repented of her former discouragement and proceeded to give her friend every hope to her wishes. Then much to Mariah's relief and as new mothers often are, Mrs Marsh was eager to change the subject and show off her new baby.

The week following Christmas was deeply unfavourable for walks and barely tolerable for carriages. But neither would Lady Coburn be talked out of having dinners nearly every evening, any more than Mariah could be talked out of attending them. Aunt Mary and Edward were welcomed also on two occasions, and though his wife was graciously invited, Elizabeth obstinately declined.

Chapter Fifteen

Early in the January, Lady Coburn was sorry that all her guests had departed from Reading and invited Mariah and Aunt Mary for supper and to look at some new music books her brother had sent her from London.

"I am always sad when they leave; we have such delightful times together," said Lady Coburn. "Frederick, of course, will be back next month," added she, particularly for Mariah's hearing. Mariah only smiled. She knew it to be true; Frederick Tenby had hinted so himself, before he had left. Mariah was gratified by the assurances of the sister and felt the warmth of their regard.

One day, several weeks later, Mariah was spending the morning above stairs. The days were still cold, wet and dull; outdoors held few prospects for pleasant occupation. Elizabeth and Aunt Mary watched on while Mariah attempted candle wicking some new bonnets for the summer when Mariah was summoned to Edward's study. The maid looked to Elizabeth hesitantly and paused before advising Mariah that the Master wished to speak with her alone. Mariah was all politeness, she smiled at Aunt Mary with some confusion, agreed to come at once and without even glancing at Elizabeth, she followed the maid out of the room. On reaching his study, he beckoned her inside.

"Please, shut the door," said Edward in a firm voice. Mariah, after doing as he bid, took a seat by him. "I've… had a letter from London," began he. Mariah looked to Edward for an explanation. "You may guess from whom, but as for myself, I confess to you now, I had no idea that he thought of you as much as that, despite my own thoughts and feelings earlier this year to you, sentiments I shared with several of our sphere, as you well know," he paused to see her face. "You know too well how we have wronged you…"

"And been forgiven, Edward."

"Nevertheless, I have concluded that I know very little of these things, and given recent events, I thought you at least ought to be consulted. So… I have decided to withhold my response till I had the chance to speak with you plainly." Mariah was intrigued and immediately assumed that the letter was from Mr Tenby. "Even now, I have no wish to send you away against your wishes."

"Of course not, Edward. I would never…" began Mariah, but Edward held up his hand to silence her.

"I shan't read you the entire letter, as there are some choicest recommendations for Elizabeth's correction, of which I might seriously consider if there is any more nonsense." He chanced a quick glance at Mariah and almost smiled. "But he also expresses a wish to see us all next month, especially you, Mariah." Mariah blushed and made no answer. "He goes on to say that his nephew will shortly follow this letter in the hopes that he will be made welcome here at Addison Terrace!" Mariah now realised the letter was from the uncle, and surprised by the application of Sir Niels, read the lines for herself. "Has the nephew made you an offer of marriage?" asked he.

"No…" Mariah shook her head.

"… Do you anticipate an offer very soon, when he comes? Do you hope for one?"

"I don't know, yes… maybe."

"Hmm!" Edward smirked. "It seems the uncle is prepared for it, even if you are not, why else would his nephew call on us? I can assure you, I have no business with the man directly he comes." Mariah returned Edward's smile. "I am very happy for you both, he is a good choice!" Mariah thanked Edward and gave her brother leave to write that they awaited the arrival of the nephew in happy anticipation and went away.

Mariah could not help but smile; she was gladdened, nay elated by this news. It took a good half hour of quietude in seclusion to tranquillise her first feelings of joy before she could re-join the others with tolerable calmness in the parlour. She did not wish to provoke Elizabeth to enquiries.

That night, she shared the news with Aunt Mary, whose tears of relief mixed with expectant joy renewed Mariah's first feelings of happiness and anticipation.

True to Sir Niels's information, Mr Tenby arrived a few days later, after calling on his sister at Chifley Grey House, unimpeded by the dreadful February weather and his cloak soaking wet from the rain. He was wholeheartedly welcomed at Addison Terrace and was offered a warm place by the fire in the parlour, while Edward, keen for they two to be alone, indelicately prompted everyone else to take up activities away from that room. This was slightly more awkward then either he or Mariah had anticipated, and she and Mr Tenby sat red faced by the fire for several moments in silence.

"You have had a wet ride. Are you warm enough? Can I get you anything for your comfort…?" asked she.

"Yes… No…" said he, pausing. "Miss Mariah… I ought to be despised by you. And yet you are more than kind… and you think well of me still. And when I learned of my supposed engagement, and I think of what might have happened," he gasped and turned away his head momentarily, "you ought to justly hate me. Yet you do not!"

"No, not at all!" declared she. "Others are to blame, not you. I knew very well it was not your plan. We spent enough time together in London to make me sure of that…! Though I did truly believe to be divided from you…" Her voice broke off and she paused long. "But it is I who should apologise, I who should be despised for my apparent contrariety, can you… can you forgive me? My hastiness was ungracious… I had no idea my brother was recovering so very much, and…"

"From what I have been told… it was hardly hasty, nor ungracious, and what else could have been done in the circumstances? No, in the light of what you understood to be the case, you have been so strong… Even now my uncle despises his hastiness to you; he cannot speak more highly of you now. I thought you above all things were brave, and especially dutiful to your aunt."

"And had it not been for Bridget…" added Mariah, "Oh… I cannot stand to think of it without sorrow, regret even…"

"Yes, I too am grateful for their interference… But come… be honest with me now, did you regard him fondly at all?" Frederick saw in her countenance that which she spoke; other than by duty, she assured him that she did not. "Then let us not delay any longer… if your feelings are as fixed as mine… my heart has always been yours…"

Mariah was heartfelt in her reply and left him in no doubt that she too had long felt the same way. It was then a brief moment from lovers to betrothed and a twinkling from betrothal to matrimony.

From the church to a wedding breakfast at Chifley Grey House with all those held dear. The couple moved to London, where Edward was often welcomed, Aunt Mary frequently stayed for the summer and her cousins in Manchester and Coventry were encouraged to call. Elizabeth, however, could never get over the advantage of her sister-in-law's marriage and refused to ever stay with them in London. And though they were always welcomed at Addison Terrace, they were never invited to stay.